Looking for Daddy's Girl

Pam Kumpe

Pam Kumpe

Copyright © 2021 Pam Kumpe

Scripture quotations are from the ESV® Bible (The Holy Bible, English Standard Version®), copyright © 2001 by Crossway Bibles, a publishing ministry of Good News Publishers. Used by permission. All rights reserved.

No part of this publication may be reproduced, distributed, or transmitted in any form or by any means, or stored in a database or retrieval system, without prior written permission of the publisher. All rights reserved.

Cover Photo: Pam Kumpe

ISBN-978-0-578-91672-9

DEDICATION

For the girl without a great father.

For the girl with a great father.

And for those who read this book—know this,
God, the Father, is looking for you.

Pam Kumpe

"The LORD bless you and keep you; the LORD
make his face to shine upon you and be gracious to you; the
LORD lift up his countenance upon you and give you peace."
Numbers 6:24–26 ESV

DISCLAIMER

Names, characters, businesses, places, events,
and incidents are either the products of the author's
imagination or used in a fictitious manner.

Any resemblance to actual persons, living or dead,
or actual events is purely coincidental.
This book is a work of fiction.

MY DADDY

Hot Days Ahead

"Not again. A dead battery and no way to call home." I tossed my cell phone to the passenger seat of the car, sighing like a spoiled little girl in a grown-up body. The outside air roared through the open windows, the noise like an airplane engine taking off. To stay awake, I needed the wind on my face, even if the humidity stuck to my skin like invisible rain, sticky and damp.

My mind raced, and each time I blinked my eyes, it was as if I turned a page from my past—the memories chasing me down the highway toward New Boston in East Texas. Shutting off my thoughts doesn't come easy for me; it's as if my brain must first run out of gas before I can calm down.

Dialing Daddy's number and hanging up has become my pattern too, for the past two years, especially when my mind won't be quiet. But when I call, I can't bring myself to talk about the hole in my heart, the one growing larger each day. I've tapped Daddy's number on my phone more times than any daughter should, only to push the red button before he answered.

Sometimes Daddy calls and checks on me, and I tell little white lies, saying life's gotten busy with writing assignments. Thus, I rush our call, and hurry the goodbye, but I always tell him how much I love him.

Last time we talked, he saw through my words because right before we hung up, Daddy said, "I'll come to stay with you. Earl could drive me."

Daddy's voice, the kindest and most loving, eased my restlessness, and it felt like a hug through the receiver. But I've spent months pushing him away, and I'm reminded I'm not the daughter he deserves, but he loves me anyway.

My heart pounded, and the tears flooded my face, making it hard to see in the dark as I drove. My soul is at a loss, so going home and being with my daddy would be great for healing my brokenness and soothing my worries. Yet, I've run away like a girl in flight at every turn. Like a paper airplane without a spot to land. My standard answer to Daddy is old news. I keep saying, "I'm fine. I have deadlines, I'm covered up. We'll talk later. I promise."

I hated hiding, and I've prayed a thousand times for God to lift me from the curb of life. To release me from the dumpster of my pain. I'm worn from wallowing in my regrets, and I've also prayed for a way to smile again. I longed to become the daughter my daddy raised, the one he called his child. Sometimes I can hear the whisper of mercy calling, reminding me how God is greater than all my sorrow, sins, and shame—a call to come home—for good.

Daddy said on the last call, weeks ago. "Please, come see me."

I choked on my words, stretching the truth. "I will and soon."

Who knew sooner would come this weekend?

My tears streamed, and I ached for my daddy's arms to wrap me up. I've disappointed him in my twenties, and now, in my late thirties. If he knew the details about my wreck, I'm not sure he'd forgive me. I've tucked the pain of that horrible night, deeper and deeper, wondering if I can forgive myself.

I gagged from replaying my brokenness, and it's like someone held their hands around my neck—squeezing, taking

8

my breath away. I tried to keep my hair out of my eyes, but the tangled mop whipped around my head like a rope. I clutched the steering wheel and shouted at the darkness. "I'm tired of being strangled by the shame. Tired of pretending."

I pushed the gas pedal, driving down the highway, ready to see Daddy. He's not in good health, and he's only sixty-six. He's too young to be sick. Goodness, I have two more hours on this interstate before I drive up to the doorstep—plenty of time to talk myself out of sharing my pain or my problems.

Besides, Daddy's lung cancer trumps my problems. This trip is for him. It's time for me to encourage Daddy, for a change.

I've questioned Earl on why he told me about the cancer and not Daddy, but he stated the time was now—for me to come home. Earl never likes keeping secrets either. So I'm sure he's informed Daddy of my situation and my losing another job.

Earl is Daddy's neighbor, fishing buddy, and lifelong friend—well, Earl's my friend too, more like a second dad. I've known him since I could toddle into the garden. Since I learned to babble.

And to think, a letter would show up in my mailbox on the heels of my temper tantrum at work, which was also my last day of employment. A letter from Earl set this trip into motion. It was perfect timing, I'd say.

I sighed, wishing to let go of my pity party. To stop the running. I'm meant to live, and I want to remember how each day is a gift. But most days, I'm frozen like a statue on display. The voices in my head remind me of how sad I am, and the shouting comes right after the wallowing. It's hard to experience peace when you're caught on the highway in the dark or stuck in the rain of yesterday's tears. It's as if I'm sitting on the curb watching others go by.

9

The roar of the bald tires slapped on the asphalt, and I stared into the night through the murky windshield, wishing I had not argued with my editor over the writing assignment. Instead, I'd compared myself to the new gal after she got the feature story—the one I expected to write. I lost myself in self-doubt, and I accused my boss of favoritism because she was young and pretty and blonde. My words slammed into the office walls, and I should have kept my opinion to myself. I regretted each sentence after the words escaped from my lips, when I silenced the newsroom.

It was the first time any of us heard the hum of the air conditioning unit rumbling in our ears, and no one talked. The other reporters and staff glared at me, and I glared at them. The awkward moment loomed, and I longed to take back my accusations.

My red hair, patchy skin, and long neck make me stand out in a crowd anyway, but it's my untamable mouth that is rude. I have far to go in being kind. If only I could rewind my day. If only I remembered before I'd spoken.

Daddy said I got Mom's temper. I do have a spirited personality, one that flares up like hot peppers when life crosses me. I'm opinionated. But trustworthy. Too loud. Stubborn. But strong. I'm not all bad. So, what's wrong with me? Oh yeah, no self-control.

Having too many opinions can be like weeds for the heart, growing wild and pumping hard. It's not the reporter's fault she received the assignment. Or the pretty genes. Or blonde hair instead of red. When will I learn that obtaining a good reference is harder when you leave a job on bad terms?

On Friday night, when I tossed the stack of envelopes onto my breakfast bar, the option to drive home became the best one. The only one I had. After all, Daddy's my lifeline and my reminder that joy exists for some people. When I'm around Daddy, he calms my anxious mind, and yet I avoid him, not wanting my discontentment to wash out his smile.

I went back to the newspaper office, handed in my keys, and packed my laptop and belongings. But of course, I'd expected to hear the words, "You're fired," anyway.

Holding a job is tough for me. Respecting authority comes harder. I'm a 38-year-old woman who can't pay my rent. I have nowhere to live. It's time to go home. Besides, Daddy needs me. Or do I need him?

After losing my husband, Kyle, and my son, Kenny, the once noisy apartment grew quieter than I could stand. So, I bought a cockatiel; the chirping was endless, and the silence was gone.

After the funeral and when the sun went down, I'd placed a bottle of whiskey on the counter. I'd stared at it, almost falling from my sobriety. But so far, I've not taken a drink. And yet, the bottle sits in the glove box of my car, in case I can't cope. In case I need to disappear and hide from life.

My mind jumped back to the funeral when Earl drove Daddy to the cemetery. Daddy's driving skills are like a monkey sitting in the seat, wild and untamed. He twists and turns and causes confusion on the road, cuts through traffic, and forgets to signal. Of course, you can't forget to signal in Dallas. But I'm not sure Earl fared much better. Earl said other drivers honked at him, but I've held on for dear life as a passenger with Earl, and he makes me nervous.

The two of them used an Atlas map Daddy saved from when he was a young man to guide them to the location, but Earl missed a turn or two, and Daddy told me they made a few U-turns, too. But they did come, even if they missed the memorial part of the service and the preacher's words about Kyle and Kenny.

The entire day of saying goodbye to my family drained the last bit of life from me. I moved when someone pointed me in a direction. I sat when another person reminded me to rest. I ate when a friend handed me a plate. I was like a remote for a TV without batteries.

Once Daddy arrived, I leaned against him, my legs like noodles, my heart succumbing to the weeds of sorrow. When I began crying at night, not able to discard the awful chapter in my life, I searched for substitutes to dull my pain.

That's when the bottle showed up on the counter, not long after the emptiness set in, when no one cried with me, when no one knew I was utterly devastated, unable to find a reason to live. However, each day the alarm reminded me to look outside because the sun was up. And then, one day, a bouquet of sunflowers arrived at my door. I knew Daddy was thinking of me. The card said, "Look at the sun. I love you."

Adding my problems to Daddy's concerns won't make his life better or brighter. But it's my turn to help him since I'm not great at pulling weeds from my life. He says there's hope in sorrow, and loss includes love, or we wouldn't hurt so much. I sure love my daddy. It's time I showed him how much.

I wiped my head, the sweat dripping beneath my bangs, the August heat not letting up. Gripping the steering wheel, staring at the interstate, I inhaled deep breaths, making myself focus on the road. A trickle of water ran down my face. *Yuck.* "Oh my, what is this? Hairspray sweat? Sticky sweat is the worst!" I spat and wiped my lips with the back of my hand. "I've never liked the heat. Never!"

My mind wandered back to my days as a girl, which included tending to the garden with Daddy, and all those trickles of sweat that never enhanced my freckles. I've watched many sunflowers bloom and picked onions, okra, hot peppers, cantaloupe, and strawberries, enjoying fresh food from the garden. Boy, do I smell like onions right now, my deodorant long gone. But I taste like hairspray!

Around the age of ten, I remember a night after picking tomatoes in the garden, Daddy scooped ice cream for us. The treat became a nightly routine after we ended our chores, giving us a chance to cool off with ice cream together in the living room.

Daddy would open the kitchen window and the living room window by the fireplace, letting the breeze blow across our damp and smudge-filled clothes. He figured ice cream solved the heartache of the day because he knew I'd hide in the garden after school, crying, when the cool kids bullied me. Most of my life, I've been a loner. I just didn't fit in.

Maybe I can bring a cool breeze of hope to his day if I remind myself to be kinder and quieter, to act like I have tape over my mouth when I might want to shout.

The memories flooded my empty life, and I found myself looking forward to seeing the old house and my daddy. When I get to New Boston, I'll stop for ice cream since Denny's is open all night. A scoop of vanilla will cool me off.

I glanced at the dark sky through the bug-strewn windshield, and the two stars that were still awake reminded me of how Daddy and I once shone together. How we used to laugh at the silly way he folded up paper to make airplanes, those he tossed at me before bedtime, or when he made breakfast. He often sailed an airplane over my head as I walked out the front door to school.

Daddy tried hard to make up for my not having a mom. She died when I was six months old, and the photos he kept are my connection to her. Daddy shows them to me when he's sad. Or when he's glad. Or anytime we're eating ice cream or making homemade jam.

I have my mom's red hair. Same freckles. Same nose. However, my nose is more extended than hers. It's grown, like my opinions. Daddy wishes I came with a pause button or an off button like a remote. I've wished for an off switch, then my mouth wouldn't get me in trouble.

As for Mom, Daddy never forgets her birthday, taking fresh flowers to her gravesite each year. I rarely say her name, Marilyn Williams. She gave me part of her name, Sally Marilyn Williams. Her birthday is August 2nd, which is a Monday. Oh, wait, is it after midnight? Yes, her birthday is today.

My fingers slid around the steering wheel, and I put my hand up to the dashboard. "Wonderful, now the air conditioner is blowing after not working earlier. It's like the heater kicked on. Nice. Everything's breaking."

I sat back, licking more hairspray and wiping the horrible taste from my tongue. "Where's a cool breeze when you need one? Or a good meal, for that matter? Or ice cream?"

I watched the two stars, in between keeping my eyes on the road. "I'll name them Max and Sally." The stars drifted over the highway in the next curve, and they appeared to hover in the sky like flying saucers. "They look like they're over our house."

I touched my growling stomach. "Instead of ice cream, I'll slip into town and go by Pitt Grill, on Highway 8. I'll order a greasy, sloppy, dripping with catsup, mustard, and mayonnaise cheeseburger. Oh, wait, what am I thinking? It's the middle of the night."

My memory of the tiny restaurant comes with nights sitting in a smoke-filled fog at the table, since you could smoke inside. Fortunately, I stopped smoking more than a dozen years ago, but the journey began back in high school when I tried to fit in with other teenage girls. I coughed and coughed and coughed, choking on that first cigarette. And they laughed, and I went to the garden and sat with the flowers, wishing for true friends.

By college, I bought my own package of cigarettes, and the journey of a thousand puffs took over my life until I met Kyle three years after I graduated with my journalism degree.

On our first date, he asked me to stop smoking, which I did. I would have done anything for him. Anything. His blue eyes pierced my entire being. His love for salads and fruit became my love, and smoking interfered with pursuing a healthy lifestyle.

After we married and we had Kenny, the whole family thing brought out the best in me. Now they're both gone, and the only family I have left is Daddy. So, he can't die. Not yet.

Touching the carton of cigarettes in the seat next to me, those I'd bought on impulse in Greenville instead of gas, I wondered if I might smoke one. But one puff, and I'd start the habit back. Besides, my daddy quit smoking when I was a baby, and he also stopped drinking. Earl once told me about how Daddy was wild as a teen and took to whiskey like many of the boys in high school, and his parents didn't sleep for four years until Daddy graduated high school.

I never saw my daddy out of control, just a whistling, jam-maker, and cook. And a lover of making paper airplanes. I never saw my daddy drink anything harder than sweet tea, either. Coffee's his morning drink, where he pours evaporated milk into his cup, more milk than coffee.

He loves bacon, scrambled eggs, and cheese toast topped with jam. With his coffee. Boy, I've missed sitting across from him at the table.

Before Daddy retired last year, he worked thirty-plus years as a cook at the downtown diner by the red light across from the new visitation center and museum. He specialized in chicken-fried steak and white gravy, loaded with a cream base. The batter included a secret ingredient, making the crust the fluffiest and tastiest.

People came from all over Texas to eat there because they knew who wore the white baker's hat in the kitchen. Yes, Daddy's old school. He wanted to look the part whenever in the kitchen. And Daddy sold his jam there, too, still does, rows of jars inside the glass counter by the register.

I'm sure he's looking forward to Pioneer Days in two weeks, where he'll set up his booth and sell *Sunflower Delights*, not so famous to the world, but famous to me and to the community. The jams are a wonderful mix of sugar and fruit and, of course, another secret ingredient. I think the component is love. But Daddy will never tell. He makes all his jams in his kitchen, from strawberry to blackberry. To peach and fig. And even watermelon.

Maybe this is an excellent time for me to cook up something—a time to find myself. I'm a little too crunchy, not tasty, but I have my sugary moments. Perhaps I'll simmer down the complex parts of my personality and let others see the softer Sally, the woman I keep tucked away. There's a part of me that longs to show mercy to a sad soul. To follow in my daddy's footsteps of loving your neighbor, not simply talking about it. Besides, I'm tired of my thoughts sinking so deep I feel like I'm drowning.

There must be an expiration date for a lousy attitude so the healing can replace the sorrow. It's time for me to remember all that I am. I want to shine again. To be whole, to rise with hope.

I tightened my grip on the steering wheel. "There's the exit." I'm hoping my hometown welcomes me to a brand-new season, one without sinking-sad days where I can find purpose. "So, which way to turn? I'm sure the Pitt Grill is closed now since it's after one in the morning."

I could barely see the dash, my eyes were dry from the hot air, and the fuel gauge showed empty. "I'd better stop for gas before heading to the house, and I'll get a snack. My destiny awaits. But it takes fuel to get there. For the car and for me."

Talking to a Dumpster

I inched the car to the pump, stopping, and looking at the price. "Wonderful, gas prices are climbing too, and I'm short on cash. My final check from the newspaper won't come until next week." I slapped my head. "I forgot to tell payroll to send my paycheck to my daddy's house. No telling when I'll get it."

The neon lights at the gas station lit up the parking lot as if daylight had snuck in on me. *Yawn!* "I'm too tired to let the day get here; I need some sleep. I'll get gas and crash in my old bed."

I glanced over my shoulder and saw a person crouched against the wall next to the ice machine, hiding in the shadows. "Who is that?" I bent to the right, peering around the pump, trying to get a closer look, wondering if my life might include sleeping in parking lots someday.

I muttered, "Poor thing. Maybe I can get that person a snack." I checked my change purse. "These ten dollars should go for gas, but five would get me home." Moving toward the store's front door, I stepped inside, scouring the racks, picking up a couple of items.

At the counter, I announced to the sleepy-eyed clerk, "Put five on pump number two, please. And I'll get these." I put the can of root beer on the counter with a granola bar.

The stone-faced man gave me the total. "That's $8.33."

I reached for a bag of chips on a nearby rack. "Add this too."

18

"That's $9.48."

I twirled around, snatching a candy bar.

The clerk grunted, "That's $9.98."

"Perfect. Can I have a bag for my items, please?"

"Sure." He sacked the granola bar, the candy, and the chips, handing me the soda.

"No, put the root beer in there, too. It's for the man outside."

"It would be best if you didn't toy with strangers. Get your gas and be on your way. I don't need you stirring things up."

"How can giving someone a snack be a problem?"

"As I said, be on your way."

"Whatever. It's just a snack." Outside, I drove my vehicle over to the curb. The shadowy man who was now staring at me pulled the hood down, glaring at me, long and intense.

I paused, whispering to the wind. "Daddy said I should be kind when life isn't kind to me." Stepping from the seat, after putting the car into park, I called, "I'm sorry you're out here tonight. Are you hungry?"

The voice cracked, "You're not sorry. I'm fine. Just leave." I stepped closer, and the shouting grew as if someone inhaled air from a helium balloon. The squeaky-pitched bark made me put the car between us. The voice cried, "Don't come any closer. You'll regret it."

"I'll regret what? Being kind?"

"You're not kind. You're showing pity. Get in that car of yours. Drive on to your perfect life." The shadow now stood, arms waving. "Go on. Get."

The breeze I'd longed for settled in on us, the air cooler, the wind strong, and the hoodie fell from the might-be-hungry person, revealing a woman near my age. She appeared a little weathered with tangled hair, but her eyes were familiar, as if an old friend hid beneath the loose jeans and the worn T-shirt.

19

I placed the snacks on the hood of the car. "You can eat this for breakfast in the morning. But if you think this is me pitying you, you're wrong. I've held a pity party in my car for the last three hours. And that party was for me. I don't have any room left in my life to feel that way toward you. I just wanted to be kind."

"Whatever you say."

I inched toward the front of the car. "What's your name? Do we know each other?"

"Do we know each other? Does it look like I run with your crowd? I'm sitting at a gas station. How many of your friends sit on curbs?"

"Can I know your name?"

The brown-haired, tan woman lunged and snatched the sack from the hood. "You don't need my name. And I don't need your pity." She hurried from the sidewalk, lugging her backpack. She didn't notice her hoodie sliding from her shoulders to the pavement.

I picked up the smudged, white jacket, and a pack of cigarettes tumbled to my feet. "These are like the ones I used to smoke. Like the ones in my car." I tossed them into the front seat, not sure why. I hated to waste a good cigarette.

I moved to the edge of the building, the woman long gone, the night heavy with a change in the air, a storm brewing, a reminder of how quickly hot air can turn to cold when a couple of clouds bump into each other.

I climbed into the car, my eyelids drooping; the nonstop craziness of packing all weekend caught up with me. My body ached as if a hammer pounded on my muscles. "I need sleep. Time to get to Daddy's house. So much for a burger or ice cream."

I pulled to the highway, the empty light a reminder of paying for the gas but not fueling my tank. "Wonderful, I never pumped the gasoline." Making a U-turn, I pulled to the pump, got out, and waved to the not-smiling clerk who peered out from inside the store. I shouted across the lot, giving him a thumbs-up. "I forgot my gas."

A wheeze of a laugh came from beside the nearby dumpster, causing me to swirl like a top. "Who's there? Is that you, my friend, the scaredy-cat from beside the ice machine?"

The dumpster talked to me. "I'm not scared. You're the fidgety one."

I paused, knowing my screaming at a dumpster might seem odd, but I was too tired to care. "Hey, I need rest. It's been a tough couple of days."

The woman hollered, "Don't call me friend. I'm no friend of yours. If I told you my name, you'd forget it by sunrise. And don't act like you know what tough is. Try being me."

I spun around, stepping into the open, my car behind me, the dumpster ahead. I was ready to argue, to defend myself, because the woman behind the dumpster challenged me. "You don't know what I've gone through either. I've put up with being overlooked at work. I'm skilled. I can write the best stories. No one understands how I see the person's heart. I do. I want to share stories filled with hope, but do you think the newspaper business sees me? Or understands me? No! They're looking for the next big news break—the story that will get the most likes on Facebook. I want to write real stories that touch hearts. But I can't. I get edited at every turn."

"Yeah, now that's a tough life. You have a job. And a car. Get over yourself."

"What? That's only a part of my story. As a baby, I lost my mom, not to mention those kids who bullied me all through school. So I left this place to find my way. Only look, now I don't have a job, and small-town life calls again."

21

"My mom and dad are gone, too. But I'm not whining about it."

"Stop telling me how I should react. You have no idea what my life looks like or how hard I'm trying to find a way to live. I just wanted to give you a snack. What's wrong with that?"

"Don't do it to make yourself feel better."

Biting my tongue, I put my hands into my jeans' pockets, trying to keep my words in, but my temper grew. I was blowing up like a hot air balloon, ready to shout. I inched closer and closer to the dumpster, my arms flailing as if they were propellers on a helicopter.

I leaned on the front of the green can, which now held some of my worries. I wiped my face of the tears, knowing I'd dumped bags of trash from my sad life on this poor soul who happened to get in my path.

A giggle rose from behind the green trash bin. "Are you crying? Nice touch."

"Never mind. You don't make it easy to be nice to you."

"Oh, go on. Wipe your face. Dry your eyes. Go home."

I popped up like a tired kangaroo. "What? So now you're giving me advice? You're the one hiding behind the dumpster."

"I'm not hiding. I know where I am and where I'm going. At least, I know where I belong."

"No one belongs out here like this."

"Hey, I'm not the one yelling into a dumpster trying to clean up my life."

"My life isn't that bad. It's mostly just sad."

"Are you listening to yourself?"

"I'm tired. That's all."

My ice machine friend yelled, "You're just trying to make yourself feel better by assuming you can clean up my life by giving me a snack."

"You've got this wrong. I just thought you'd be hungry."

"I'm not. I was asleep until you woke me up. And why are you raising your voice? I can hear you just fine."

I stepped back, unable to answer or think, longing for a piece of my heart to live and soar. I whispered, trying not to yell, "Why does everything have to be so hard?"

The breeze sent my hair across my face, and it appeared as though the two lids on the top of the dumpster were flapping, making fun of me. Bullies at night. Bullies at work. Bullies around me—a shadowy bully behind the dumpster.

A call from behind me sent me stumbling. The clerk hollered, "Are you all right, lady? As I said earlier, I don't need trouble. Do I need to call for help?"

A cackle from behind the dumpster said, "Lady, are you all right?"

I grimaced, yelling at the trash bin. "Don't mock me."

The man held up his cell. "I'm calling the police if you don't leave."

The dumpster voice added, "He'll call the police, and they'll arrest you. You're acting a little crazy, I'd say."

I inched closer to the lean but stern-faced man, my hands waving, offering a humble, regretful hug. "I'm sorry. I haven't had any sleep. I've driven for hours, and I lost my job on Friday. I don't have but a few dollars on me. I need rest. I need a pillow for my head. I need …" I touched the tear on my face.

The clerk said, "Lady, you might need to talk to someone."

"I have been talking, but nobody is listening to me. And it's my mother's birthday. She died right after I was born. And I want my daddy. He lives on Front Street in the little white house with the garden of sunflowers. So just let me go." My rambling took over; my sense of losing control and babbling sounded like hot air blowing from the dash of my heart, like a busted air-conditioning unit.

I sighed, taking in tiny breaths, glancing at every corner of the parking lot. I noticed the clerk stood with his hands on his hips, and my eyes cut back to the dumpster, where silence hung like raindrops trickling from the sky as thunder rumbled, sending a downpour. Finally, marching to the front of the store on the heels of the clerk, I apologized, "It's been rough lately. I'm so sorry."

"Be on your way. One more outburst, and I'm calling the police."

As rain fell, I rushed to the car with each clap of thunder, getting soaked like a fish swimming between the pelting raindrops. Beneath the awning at the pump, I put gas into my car and waved at the man inside the store. "I'm leaving. I'm so sorry."

Embarrassed by my behavior, I crawled into the car.

While looking down, I noticed the dome light was on even though I'd shut the door, and the carton of cigarettes was no longer in the seat. "No way! The glove box is open, too." I rummaged around in the papers. The bottle of whiskey was missing for sure, and the passenger door was cracked open. Thus, the reason the light didn't turn off.

"Wonderful, that woman snuck over and took my cigarettes and her pack." I peered into the back seat. "She grabbed her hoodie too."

Sighing, I reached across the front and pulled the door closed, my car barely big enough for short people, let alone normal-sized ones. I rubbed my throbbing temples on my head, consumed by how the past hour zapped the rest of my energy. I asked myself, "How does a simple act of kindness turn into another session of me explaining myself to a stranger? And why would she steal from me?"

I hugged the steering wheel, heading for Daddy's house. "I'm too tired to report the theft to the police, but that woman took my whiskey. I've kept it since the funeral, in case I finally broke into pieces, like slivers of glass. She also took my brand-new carton of cigarettes, not that I needed them. And boy, did she seem familiar. I think I know her, but I'm not sure how."

Paper Airplanes

Sitting in the idling car in the driveway, I wished I'd come home more often. It's as if I'm visiting a distant relative. Each time I see Daddy, we spend days getting reacquainted, learning each other's routines. He gets up early. I want to sleep late. He wins by whistling in the kitchen and by turning up the country music on the radio.

The rain poured a coolness over the county. My feet were wet, and my hair was dripping with water. But I no longer tasted the nasty hairspray running down my face. Instead, the rain rinsed the soot from my weekend, offering a freshness I've missed. A house with memories awaited my return.

I remember how dusty the sunflowers get and how a summer rain wipes the layer of dirt from the stalks and flowers, exposing a brighter yellow and a sparkling green landscape of beauty. And the vegetable plants get a nice drink too. When the mask of dirt gets removed, the plants thrive. If my wake of sorrow gets washed away, maybe I will grow into the person whom God smiles upon.

The low spot beside the steppingstones created a small lake in the front yard, and the puddle appeared deep enough to sink a grown person. If I jumped into the middle, would I dissolve into nothingness? I hopped and hopped like a small girl from my youth, bathing in the muddy water. And thankfully, I didn't drown.

I hurried back to the car, opened the door, and lifted my backpack from the seat. "My purse is in this bag, along with my laptop. And tomorrow I'll get a charger since my phone's dead. My clothes are in the suitcases in the trunk, and I'll get those later. I have clothes in the dresser in my room. Or Daddy will lend me something to wear."

My lips stuck together from too much talking, and I replayed my scene at the gas station where I screamed at the dumpster. I'm glad the clerk didn't call the police station. But I couldn't help but wonder, why didn't the thief take my backpack from the car too?

I slung my bag over my shoulders and inched myself to the porch. The screen creaked, and the heavy door added its high-pitched noise, reminding me that no one sneaks up on Daddy. "Sunflower, what are you doing? It's after two in the morning. Earl told me you were coming, and I've called your phone ten times. All I got was your voicemail. You are old enough to return your dad's call. I've been worried you had a wreck or worse."

I ignored his put-out tone, offsetting his words with a grin. "My phone is dead, and I've lost my charger. But Daddy, you look great. You don't look sick." I patted his undershirt-belly, the one probably full of late-night ice cream, and then I danced around him, hugging him from the back, the side, the front, and then the other side. "Daddy, you're in your underwear."

He glanced down. "I live here, Sunflower. This is how I sleep."

"No one calls me Sunflower anymore. Sally is fine."

"I'll call you Sunflower until the flowers don't bloom."

"Daddy, please. I'm thirty-eight. Call me Sally."

He touched my arm. "Why did it take you so long to get here?"

"I packed up my clothes and dropped off the bird. You know my cockatiel, Angel, she's not good with moves, so she'll stay with a neighbor. I borrowed a friend's truck and paid two guys to move my furniture into storage on Saturday, and then on Sunday, I carried stuff to the dumpster and packed the rest of my belongings. Time got away, and I drove out of Dallas after dark." I paused with my rambling. "Can I stay awhile? Things are tough for me right now."

"Did you get let go from the paper?"

"Wait, why would you ask me about my job?"

"Your friend who is keeping Angel called. She thinks your bird misses you already. And she caught me up on your week and how it ended."

"Nice, Nancy can be a pain, a nosey one for sure."

"I'm sure she's not much worse than you."

I grinned. "Yeah, you're right. But as for my job, I would have gotten fired if I hadn't let myself go. Daddy, my life's complicated. The last two years have felt like a continuous tsunami, wave after wave. Problems follow me."

"Sunflower, we all deal with problems. Maybe you're causing a few of those waves to heighten and grow. But, sometimes, a wave is just a wave."

"I have trouble knowing how I should react to my problems."

"You can hit pause and not scream. Don't you usually raise your voice when you get upset?"

"Sometimes." I hugged his neck. "I'm not screaming now. I'm calmer, well, maybe a little wet, but too tired to holler at anyone."

"Where are your clothes? You're wetter than a chicken caught outside the coop in the rain."

"In the car. I'll get them when we get up."

"Go find one of my T-shirts and a pair of sweatpants."

"I have some old clothes in my dresser."

"No, you don't. I donated your clothes to someone."

"Okay, that was nice of you," I grumbled, wondering why he gave my items away. I've kept clothes in this house since high school.

Daddy broke my frown. "You know you're welcome here. Earl told me he mailed you a letter last week about my doctor's visit. But don't worry, cancer's not stopping me. What time I have left, I plan to work for the Lord."

"I'm here as long as you need me." *Crunch.* Bending over, I wrapped my fingers around a paper airplane. "Daddy, look at this room. You must have made thirty paper airplanes. It's like a rug of paper in here."

"As it got late, and when I kept calling, I'd fold up the paper and send it across the room while I watched reruns of Billy Graham, the old ones that are in black and white. I kept praying you'd show up every time I sent one soaring. I waited for you to fly into the house. But then I fell asleep and woke up to this storm. It rarely rains like this in August."

I was glancing around the familiar landscape of the dark green plaid couch and Daddy's favorite recliner, the comforts of home. I marched through the open double doors into the dining room. "I see you have your jam ready for the festival. You can't even sit at this table."

"Yes, I've got them grouped by the kind of fruit. The labels go on the jars tomorrow. But first, I'm going to visit your mother in the morning. It's her birthday. Do you want to ride with me?"

"I'm not so sure. Maybe." Yawning, I wiped my eyes. "Daddy, let's get some rest. This rain will put us fast asleep."

Daddy touched my shoulder. "You might need to shake out the dust on the quilt on your bed. I don't clean much in there unless Earl reminds me."

I sighed, the relief of safety settling in my heart. "Where's Snowball? He usually jumps on me and meows." I turned to Daddy. "You do have him, don't you?"

"Well, I have a new cat. But it's fine. I named this cat Snowball, too."

"Is he black?"

"Yes, I like black cats. They're easy to spot in the daylight. And they can sneak around and get the mice at night when it's dark."

"How many cats have you taken in?" I didn't wait for his answer and hurried back to the living room toward the door leading to my old bedroom. "Four cats, right?"

He bellowed through the walls. "No, this is number five. At least since you graduated high school, it seems my cats run off like my daughter. But I keep replacing them with new ones."

"Well, I didn't run away. I grew up, went to college, and stayed in Dallas after graduating. I'm not a kid anymore. So please don't go and replace me. You have one daughter, don't forget."

"But a visit now and again would be good."

"I know. Time gets away."

**

Standing in front of my dresser, I touched the photos from my youth that were taped on the mirror. "My word. I need to get rid of these or pack them up. There's me at Wright Patman Lake with Daddy near the spillway on a day we fished for hours. I'm reading and sitting in a lawn chair since I've never liked fishing, but I wanted to go with him. I must have been eight or nine."

Daddy always carried a small camera with him and developed photos every month to show me how wonderful and fortunate we were to have each other. That's when my love for taking photographs started, me smiling for Daddy as I sat in my lawn chair. Or by a sunflower. Or on the couch.

I glanced at the other pictures, one of me roller skating at the pavilion downtown and another with me next to the Christmas tree in the dining room when I was around fifteen. That's the year the first Snowball attacked a box of chocolates and knocked over the tree when we were at church. After that, Snowball got banished from the house, and he started sleeping on the grill in the backyard. I'm glad he never jumped up there when the grill was hot with charcoal.

Pulling the covers back, after changing into Daddy's clothes, I crawled under the sheets, not checking for dust on the orange and blue quilt. I hollered, "Night, Daddy." The dusty memories were great material for dreaming. I blinked hard, and my eyelids closed.

I could hear Daddy in his bedroom as his footsteps stomped on the hardwood floor. There's no hallway in the house. To get from room to room, you make a big circle. And you'll end up where you started if you keep walking.

I sang, "Night, Daddy. See you in the morning."

"Night, but it's early morning now. I'll be up in three hours. Earl's coming over to get me. He's going to drive me to the cemetery."

"Don't get me up. I'm sleeping until noon."

"Sunflower, sleeping away the day won't make your joy come back. So get up with the chickens and meet the sunrise. I've got rows of sunflowers in the garden, and they face the east and move like a dial with the sun. Get moving and follow the sun."

"Thanks, Daddy, but I'll look at the flowers when I wake up." I wiped my nose of yesterday's worries and wanderings. Daddy's way of talking about his sunflowers always meant he was talking about following Jesus, not the sun in the sky.

Birthday Celebration

"What time is it?" I rolled over, pulled the quilt and sheets over my head, and curled into a ball, hiding beneath the covers. A few more minutes of sleep. Sleeping in on a Monday might become a new goal.

Meow. Meow.

I shoved the sheets and the quilt off. "Snowball?"

The softest, blue-eyed kitty gazed at me. "Wait, you're not black? You're whiter than milk straight from the cow. So why would Daddy say you're black?"

Meow. Meow.

I hollered, "Daddy, are you up? Are you here?" Rubbing Snowball's ears, I kissed the top of his head, but he twitched and jumped from the bed, scampering from the bedroom. "It's nice to meet you, too, Snowball."

Shuffling to Daddy's room, his unmade bed told me he was out and about, so I moved to the front door, after grabbing my keys, and stood on the front porch in my bare feet. "Yep, Daddy's truck is gone. He's probably visiting Mom."

I admired how tall the two Mimosa trees had gotten, one to my right, one to my left. They've grown up with me. Now I'm shorter than the trees. The sidewalk stretched from the front door to the curb, straight to a black mailbox. "That's new. When did Daddy put that there?"

I scrunched mud between my toes, trekking to my car, the ground wet from the rain. But the sun shone brightly, low in the eastern sky. "What time is it? I've got to get a charger and charge my phone."

Hurrying, I made three trips, unloading my trunk while sloshing in the mud and tracking dirt into the house. Daddy's airplanes were stacked off to the side as if they were waiting for a flight. I picked one up, sending the paper airplane toward the dining room, where it landed on the thirty or more jars of jam.

As I shoved my suitcases across the floor toward my room, I wiped my toes on a towel from the bathroom, knowing a bath was in order before getting dressed. I glanced down. "I'd better mop the floor before Daddy sees the mess in the living room, too."

Meow. Meow.

"Hi, Snowball. Daddy might not want you on the table. But wait, you're an outside cat. Did you slip in when Daddy left?"

The cat meowed while prancing around on the top of the jam as if toying with me. I marched to the kitty. "Get down, before you knock off a jar. You don't want to deal with the wrath of a redhead."

Snowball bounced to the floor, slipping and sliding like a kitty wearing roller skates, and he skidded over the kitchen floor. I trotted behind him as if I were shoveling snow, and he scampered across the screened-in porch toward the patio door. "Go on now."

I opened the screen, and he hurried to the garden, where sunflowers towered with yellow blooms, painting the edge of the garden with gold and brown beauties.

Turning around, I nearly ran into the makeshift bed. "What's this? A cot on Daddy's porch? Maybe he gets tired and sleeps out here."

Back in the kitchen, the clock read 9:45 a.m. "Why am I up? Maybe I can catch Daddy at the cemetery. I'll run by the florist on Elm Street and buy flowers. I've never taken any to my mom before, so I'll get something pretty, like violets."

I put my hands on my hips, taking a deep breath. "It's a new day. I'll stand tall and face the day like Daddy, with a trust in God. He's content with jam, his cat, and sunflowers. And with paper airplanes. I could use some of his contentment."

Sticking my feet into the tub, I washed off my toes. A bath will wait, and a ponytail will work for now. I threw on my jeans and a top, then danced around the mud to the car, not wanting to get my other tennis shoes wet.

At the florist, the angled parking put me almost in front of the door. Daddy's truck sat a couple of spaces over, the dingy-gray pickup with miles and miles left in it. With miles and miles of toting me around as a girl.

I snuck into the shop, carrying my debit card, knowing my checking account balance was less than $100, so shopping for small, cheap items was in order. I stood next to the birthday card selection, keeping an eye on Daddy, who hummed and seemed to love shopping for Mom.

I was spying on him, and it was nice to see his love for Mom in action. I eavesdropped, taking in his smile as he held a dozen red and white roses and a card, along with a red and silver helium 'I love you' balloon.

Pretending to select a card, I read one, put it back, picked another, and held it close, all the while watching Daddy celebrate his purchases. Daddy told the clerk, "It's Marilyn's birthday. She's waiting for me. And boy, does she love roses."

The cashier dropped the change into Daddy's hand, and he two-stepped his way from the florist shop. I slid behind a rack, relishing a side of my daddy lost in the miles, where memories kept him singing.

The clerk told the other employee, "Max loves his wife better than most men. Too bad Marilyn isn't alive."

A tear rolled down my cheek, and I clutched a card while holding a small pot of violets. I hopped to the counter, and the clerk with wispy bangs asked, "Don't I know you? But wait, don't answer. You're Sally Williams. That was your dad." She motioned to the door. "Wait, aren't you together?"

"It's Sally Snow, not Williams. I'm going to surprise my daddy by going to the cemetery with him. I arrived late last night, and he's not expecting me to be awake."

Wispy bangs spoke, "We went to high school together. It's been years, but I remember your blue eyes and red hair, and ..."

I filled in the rest of what she didn't say. "And you remember my temper."

"Well, maybe. Your personality did stick out in a crowd."

"I'm working on doing better. So, what's your name? I don't remember you."

"It's Penny. I bought the store a few years ago. I love to make floral arrangements, and this shop was for sale."

"Well, good to see you. Take care."

"Come see us anytime."

**

I parked in the shade of the oak trees next to the Red Bayou Methodist Church, and I opted to give Daddy time at Mom's marker at the cemetery. I held my card, not signed, but the birthday wishes for more birthdays applied, sort of, a not-so-great choice of a card when a person is in the grave. But this is the first card I'd ever bought for Mom. So, it will have to do.

The miniature violets, purple like my shoes, were my favorite color, and I wondered what Mom's favorite things might have been besides red-and-white roses. Clutching the potted plant, I listened to Daddy's private talk beside the fence. "Happy Birthday, Hon. Guess who came to town for your party?" He touched the tombstone as if she listened to him, and then he leaned closer as if listening to her.

He then outlined her name on the marker with his finger. "That's right, Sunflower's home. Maybe she'll stay in New Boston. At least, I'm praying."

A blob of tears streamed down my face, and I glanced at my purchase, my violets paling in comparison with the flowers Daddy placed next to Mama's resting spot.

Daddy held up the birthday card. "Honey, I'll read this to you. You'll love what it says, but let me open the envelope. Oh, can I sit by you? I woke up tired this morning. The doctor said to expect some changes. I'm ready to see you whenever my time is up. But I long for some time with Sunflower too. Maybe I'll take her fishing."

I trekked up. "Hey, Daddy, can I sit with you? I'd love to hear what Mom's card says."

Daddy fumbled and stumbled, caught off guard. "You scared me. I thought I was alone. Earl was coming with me, but he forgot to set his alarm, and he slept in this morning."

"At least someone is getting some sleep." I covered my mouth. "Sorry, I didn't mean to be rude. I didn't mean to frighten you either. I got Mom a present for her birthday, too. See." I held up the violets and my card.

"Come sit with me in the grass. I'm sure I'll need help getting up. These legs get stiff."

"Sure, let's have a party."

Daddy went down slowly, holding onto the marker, and I plopped cross-legged next to him, placing my plant next to his flowers. "Hi, Mom. Happy Birthday." I looked at the ground. "Are we sitting in ants?"

"No, if we were, you'd know it."

"Good, I don't miss the ants."

Daddy shook his head and proceeded to read his card. "Hon, this is a card written for you by someone else. But I like what it says. So listen to the words."

I sighed, unable to get comfortable because the sadness inside my heart made my bottom side heavy like a rock. I shuffled to my knees. "Sorry, go on."

Daddy raised his eyebrows. "Are you comfortable now?"

"Yes, for now." I wiggled for another reason, too, because I've never visited Kyle or Kenny's gravesites since their funeral. And right now, I wish I could drive to Dallas and talk to them like Daddy talks to Mom. But, instead, I found myself praying, silently. "God, thank you for my family. I tend to forget what's important."

Daddy broke the silence of my wandering mind, the one praying at a birthday party. He spoke with a soft tone. "Hon, here we go. The card says I will love you forever. You're my best friend. We can weather any storm. Because we're together." He placed the card next to the flowers, running his finger along the tombstone, which spelled out her name.

I cleared my throat to keep from crying. "Daddy, that's sweet."

"I would rather save the money and buy worms and take her fishing. She loved fishing and waiting for the big one. But I can't..." Daddy took a breath, coughing.

"Are you okay?"

"Yeah, this party always ends sadder than when it begins."

"I'll go fishing with you today. How does that sound?" I choked on those words, but somehow, the strangling cleared up faster when Daddy started to sing, "Happy birthday to you.

37

Happy birthday to you. Happy birthday, dear. We love you so much."

My watery eyes gave me away, and my words confirmed my curiosity. "When did you start singing? You barely opened your mouth in church when I was younger."

"I sing to your mom. She's missed so much. She doesn't cringe when I sing either."

Sighing, I reached for Daddy's hand. "I think I've missed too much, myself. I'm so glad to be here with you."

Daddy squeezed my hand, his aging spots darker than I remembered, but the smile on his face fresh with hope. His eyes were red from the tears, though, but he never runs out of grins for me or anyone.

"Sunflower, help me up. I've got a list of things to do for Pioneer Days, labels to put on the jars, and to check whether the canopy is rotted. Might need a new one for the booth. Let's not waste the day."

I balanced on my legs and helped Daddy from the ground, but his knees buckled, and he grabbed his chest, falling forward, squishing Mom's roses like an ax chopped them down.

"Daddy, are you okay? Daddy?" I crawled closer to his face, rolling him over. "Daddy?"

"I can't catch my breath." He held his hand over his chest.

Daddy's fingers let go of the ribbon, and the balloon drifted higher and higher to the puffy clouds. I prayed, "Dear God, don't take my daddy. I need him. Please, let him stay."

Prowler or Dumpster Girl

After reviewing some of the tests and taking more blood, the doctor's explanations included Daddy staying in the hospital for observation. They wanted to make sure he was stable and breathing better before they let me take him home.

Daddy responded, sitting halfway up in the bed, "Let me sleep at home. Sunflower, my daughter, can watch me. I won't rest up here."

The doctor patted his arm as if they had had discussions like this, those Daddy loses. The nurse poked and prodded, recording his vitals on her computer-on-wheels.

"I could go home. My blood pressure is good. My blood is running through my veins. I'm better now. Just had a spell."

I piped in, "Daddy, let them get you stronger. Rest for a day. It will be good for you."

"So now I'm taking advice from my wandering daughter." He smiled, and his eyes brightened when we made eye contact.

Daddy had become more alert right before the ambulance arrived, and I had followed behind them to Texarkana in my car. I was thankful for the bit of gasoline in my tank, and the drive was the longest 22 miles of my life.

To get the first responders to the cemetery, I flagged a car down on Highway 8. The driver phoned for help, thinking I was on drugs or crazy when I ran onto the highway. It took a little explaining before he made the call. But the man stayed with me until the EMTs arrived, and the guy assured me he'd buy some of Daddy's jam at Pioneer Days because Daddy was kind to him many years ago.

I kissed Daddy on the head. "I'm going home. I'll check on you later."

"Just come back for me. That's all I ask."

"I will. I love you."

"Love you too, Sunflower."

Daddy gave me his rehearsed instructions for labeling the jars of jam, a task that became mine. "Press the sticky part of the label onto the jar and use the blue marker to write which kind of jam is inside. I want my buyers to purchase the right flavor."

"Yes, sir. I can make labels stick. Surely."

"Be sure to write with the gold marker *Sunflower Delights* by Max Williams on the top of each label, too."

"That's going to take forever." I mouthed, catching myself before I said too much. "Sorry, I've got it. I'll get this done for you. I promise."

"I like things done a certain way."

"I'll make the labels look perfect."

"Nothing's perfect. Just do your best."

"Yes, sir." I wiggled in my shoes like a toddler with big feet. "Daddy, I can do this."

He mumbled, something he rarely does. "Make them look nice."

"I will. You stay in this bed and listen to the doctor. You don't have to be perfect. Just do your best to follow their instructions."

He grinned. "Stop using my words on me. You know I'd rather go home."

I patted his arm, and the blur of being in a hospital room with my only living relative sent waves of confusion through me. It's as if I stood on a grill with burning charcoal and sank into ashes of sorrow, hissing on the inside like a mad kitty whose paws were on fire. I swallowed hard, hating how certain moments trigger panic and anxiety, engulfing my whole body.

"Bye, Daddy. I'm off to label the jars."

I pulled up to the house after making a stop at Walmart for a charger, and Earl, the skinniest man alive, almost, met me in the yard. He and Daddy made quite the pair. They're like Laurel and Hardy, one thick and one long. Daddy's heavier and shorter, and his thinning gray hair shows most of his head, while Earl sports the blackest hair, and he's towering at over six feet.

I stepped out of the car, hugging the friend-neighbor of my youth, who was also a family friend of Daddy's before I was born. "Earl, my daddy's going to live, right? How sick is he?"

"Girl, no one is ready to say goodbye to a loved one. Let the doctors check him out. He'll be home in a few days." Earl brushed my bangs from my face as he used to when I was a youngster. "Do you need anything? Have you eaten?"

"I'm fine. I'm going to label Daddy's jars. That will make him happy, knowing I'm obeying him for a change."

Earl motioned. "I'll be over there on the porch if you need me. Or inside if I get too hot."

"Thank you. We'll need to get Daddy's truck later. It's at the cemetery."

"Let me know when you're ready. My day is pretty open. And it's so great to see you home."

"Thank you." I marched inside, carrying my sack with the new phone charger, and I stopped a foot into the living room, almost before I got my entire body inside. I lost my breath. "And who are you?"

A black cat stretched his back into an upside-down arch on the back of the couch, exposing his claws.

I threw up my hands, the crunching of my sack startling the cat. "Wait, you were white this morning." I paused, rubbing my eyes, the lack of sleep falling on me like a low ceiling in an old house. "I'm more tired than I thought."

Meow. Meow.

"Snowball?"

Meow. Meow.

The cat pounced to the floor, rubbing up against my legs like a rubber band, bending and curling around my feet, and purring.

"Well, you're nicer in the afternoon. Maybe you wake up grumpy like me." I bent down, petting Snowball. "I could swear you were white this morning."

Meow.

"Well, Daddy has left me with a task. So let's get to it."

After I placed Snowball on the arm of the couch, he settled in on the perch, watching me with his green eyes. "I'll be right back. I've got to charge my phone."

Digging in my backpack, I poured lipstick, a compact, my contact solution, and a voice recorder onto the unmade bed, followed by my laptop. "Where is my phone?"

I fell back onto the bed, the softness inviting. I could doze off in a minute. But I promised Daddy I'd get those labels put on the jar. Forcing myself to stand, I fished inside my purse. "There's my phone. I've had it with me the entire time. I could have charged it in the car on my way to the house."

Kerplunk! Plunk!

"Earl, is that you?" I slipped into the living room where Snowball slept, and he curled into a ball of silky fur. "Earl? Hello?"

From the back of the house, somewhere near the kitchen, another *kerplunk* came with a shout, and Snowball shot up on all fours, peering over the jars of jam.

I hesitated to speak but did anyway. "Boy, what is it? Earl, please answer."

A voice hollered, not responding to me. "Darn it. Come on, Charcoal, we've got to help Max. I can't chase you right now. We're here to work."

I ran to the front door, onto the porch, and charged across the driveway to the right. "Earl? Are you there?"

His face turned toward me from his porch swing. "Sally, what's got you stirred up?"

I hurried, rushing like a spooked cow. "There's someone in the back of Daddy's house. It's a woman. I heard her voice. Does Daddy have someone come to the house to clean?"

"No, little lady. I'm his reminder to clean. Your dad is good at washing pots and pans and his clothes, not dusting or mopping floors."

"Call the police. We have a prowler."

"A prowler? It's probably Ruby."

"Who is Ruby?" My tone snapped like a lightning strike, fast and quick.

Earl leaned over the rail. "Max hires her to help with the garden. To deliver eggs to the neighbors for him. To get his booth ready for Pioneer Days. To deliver jam when he has a big order. She's a hard worker and a better friend than most people."

I pondered his words, unsure if Ruby was an old lady or someone taking advantage of Daddy. "Are you sure? We should call the police. I heard her talking to someone named Charcoal." I hopped in the driveway, avoiding a mud puddle to get closer to Earl.

Earl joined me, his giraffe legs bringing him to my side. "Come with me. I'm sure it's Ruby. I thought your dad told you about her. He's pretty attached to Ruby."

I grimaced. "Daddy's not getting married to Ruby, is he?"

"Married? I don't think so." He chuckled, gasping as if I said something funny.

We moved into the house, Earl went first, and I peeked from behind him. Earl called, "Ruby, is that you?"

"Yeah, it's me. I'm in Max's bedroom."

I tugged on his arm, whispering, "She's in Daddy's bedroom?"

"I'm sure she has a reason. Max trusts her completely." Earl rubbed Snowball's head as he walked by him on the sofa. "Ruby, I've got someone for you to meet. By the way, Max isn't here. He collapsed at the cemetery, and he's in the hospital for observation."

"Is Max going to be all right?" The voice came closer, first from near the bathroom, then from my bedroom, as the woman kept talking. "I hope so." The yapping stranger walked into the living room. "Max asked me last week to come by today and do the labels."

A shadow of a late-night person, the one wearing a white hoodie, halted, almost leaving skid marks on the hardwood floor in her gray tennis shoes. The shirt she wore looked familiar, like my striped, green T-shirt. She cradled a white cat, and her voice screeched in a pitch no soprano could match. "Earl? Who is she? That can't be. No way."

I stepped around my giraffe friend as she pointed at me, and as I pointed my finger at her. "So, you're my daddy's friend? You? The person who sleeps on curbs at night. You?"

"Stop judging me. You don't know one thing about me."

"I know enough to wonder why you're in my daddy's bedroom. I know you stole my cigarettes and my whiskey."

Ruby raised her eyebrows, her long brown hair bouncing in the ponytail. "So, you're Sally Snow? You look different in the daytime and when you're not whining about something.

44

You're the Sally who never comes home to see her dad, who disappeared down the highway." Her tiny mouth matched her squinty eyes as she made a rather annoying slur of my name. "Sally, the wayward daughter."

Earl's eyes widened, his mouth hanging open. "Ruby, wait. Have you two met?" He turned to me. "And Sally, you stopped smoking years ago after you graduated from rehab. Are you drinking again?"

"No, I'm not smoking or drinking. I had a carton of cigarettes in my car, and the whiskey was hidden in my glove box in case of an emergency. Little Miss Ruby helped herself to both last night."

Ruby placed the white cat on Daddy's recliner. "I never touched your cigarettes or your whiskey. I took my hoodie back and my pack of cigarettes. That's all."

My temples throbbed as an explosion erupted inside my brain. "So, you're telling me that you never touched my stuff, only yours?"

"That's right. I saw you pick up my jacket and toss it into your car. When you were explaining yourself to the store clerk in the parking lot, I grabbed my things and took off."

"You didn't take off. You were behind the dumpster."

"I was there for part of your yelling. But not all of it."

"So, who took my cigarettes and the bottle?"

"Well, they do have cameras at the gas station. I bet you can find out. But you'll be surprised. It's not me." Ruby put her hands into her pockets as if to keep from swinging at me. She added, "By the way, the reason I was in the bedroom was that Charcoal darted inside with me. He hid under your dad's bed. And Max likes the cats outside."

"Well, you must have let him inside."

"He darted inside. I never invited him. You're making this hard to explain."

I did a double-take, realizing, in my shock, that Ruby and I met at the gas station during the night. I was relieved that I wasn't losing my mind; there were indeed two cats. One white, Charcoal. And one black, who must be Snowball.

Earl waved his spaghetti arms like a referee as if trying to back us into the corner of the boxing ring. "Ladies, let me reintroduce you to each other. It sounds like you need a fresh start."

Meoooow.

Snowball arched his back and pounced on Charcoal, and their claws, along with the horrible meows, mimicked the arguing Ruby and I displayed, and they stretched their vocals into roars.

Ruby rushed for Charcoal, and Earl snatched up Snowball. "Ladies, let's call a truce. Your behavior has set these cats against each other."

I marched to the dining room table with Earl behind me, and I ran my fingers in circles on the lids of the jams, whispering to him, "I don't understand. Daddy never mentioned Ruby."

Ruby tramped up, standing across the table, wrapping her arms around the growling white cat. She offered her two cents. "Well, your dad mentioned you, and he spoke of you as if you were in a foreign land or something."

I stormed across the room. "I'm not in a foreign land. I'm right here."

"Then why haven't you come to see Max?"

"Now you're meddling?"

Earl took her side. "Sally, your dad would love to see you more."

I growled at both of them. "Stop trying to make me feel guilty for staying away."

46

Ruby responded, "Guilt is a sign of wrongdoing. If the shoe fits, wear it."

Earl shook his head. "Ruby, no need for such comments."

They put the cats on the floor, and I picked up a jar of strawberry jam, investigating the contents with a keen eye. "I've been busy. Work. Writing. Worrying."

Ruby mocked. "But not worried enough to come home. I've known Max for almost two years, and he's like the dad I wished for when I was small. Yet, in all this time, you haven't once stepped inside this house. So, tell me, how busy have you been?"

I argued, "Don't get too confident. If you're so close, why didn't Daddy tell me about you?"

Earl motioned for Ruby to sit on the couch in the other room, and he shuffled, showing me where to sit opposite her. "Ladies. We need to stop this. It's not helping. The bickering is a sign of unresolved issues."

I added, "Nothing's unresolved." I sat down but jumped right back to my feet, bouncing myself to the kitchen. "And where are those labels?"

Ruby charged the other way, through my room, circling by the bathroom. She bellowed, "I'll get the labels. It's my job to label the jam."

As we circled inside the house, we nearly collided at the back porch. I held out my hand. "Give me the labels. Daddy assigned me the task."

"No, Max hired me last week."

"He's *my* daddy." My hands were on my hips.

"But he's my friend."

"He's always going to pick me first." I scowled, holding my hand out, snapping my fingers.

Ruby placed her hand behind her back. "I'm not giving you these labels."

Earl called to us from the dining hall. "Hush, both of you. The phone's ringing."

We rolled our eyes at each other but honored Earl, which put us side by side in the doorway leading from the kitchen, facing Earl. He picked up the receiver. "Yes, this is Earl Milton. I'm a neighbor. Sure, Sally's here. Let me get her."

Earl passed the receiver to me. "Yes, this is Sally." I listened to the words from the doctor, whose sentences sent a sadness deep into my soul. I mustered up a small response. "I understand. Metastasized? To other parts of his body? Yes, I know what that means. Please, tell him I love him."

Unable to stay in the house, my throat tightened, and I couldn't say another word. I tore past Earl and Ruby, dropping the receiver. I couldn't let them see my cry.

Outside, I piled into the middle of the garden, which took up most of the side yard and a large part of the back, except for Daddy's shop and the chicken coop.

Plopping myself into the mud, hiding between the stalks of green, I wallowed in despair, and yet, I was unable to rise from the murky sadness. I wept, "Why did I tell the doctor I understood? I don't. My daddy can't be this sick."

Of Okra and Sunflowers

Sitting in the mud in the middle of the afternoon isn't how I planned to spend my mom's birthday. Yet, here I am. The towering sunflowers were oblivious to my squatting in their garden, but the reality of the last couple of days has me overwhelmed, to the point of taking my anger out on Ruby.

The sunflowers faced the sun in the west, making me almost smile as I pondered Daddy's words about following the sun. Daddy's right about having faith and trust in God, but I'm struggling. And now I'm jealous of Ruby, who is inside my house.

Tears landed in the mud, and I couldn't tell which puddle was full of sorrow or simply holding guilt and anger.

The patio screen door bounced with a bang, and Ruby called, "What did the doctor say? You ran from the house without a word. When Earl took the phone, the doctor was gone. He called your dad's room, and no one answered. Hello, a little information would be good. You're not the only person who loves Max."

I screamed at the top of my lungs. "My daddy's worse than I realized."

"You don't have to yell at me. I can hear you. The chickens can hear you. The entire neighborhood can hear you. Details. I want details. Doctors can be wrong."

"Or they can be right."

Earl spoke. "Sally, come and talk to us."

"No, I'm good, right here."

"Sally, your dad's a fighter. We'll take it one day at a time."

I didn't answer and splashed my hand in a puddle, ready to rip down every flower within reach. But they were Daddy's pride and joy, so I refrained. If Kyle were here, he'd hold me. And I would let him. But right now, the pain is ripping me apart, the idea of losing my daddy swallowed up my breath and my strength.

I spoke to the okra plants, those wilting from the humidity and heat. "Kyle was my rock. He was my constant. He was all I needed." I flicked the leaf of the plant with my finger. "Are you listening to me?"

Outside the garden, on the edge, Ruby whispered, "Earl, she's worse off than you told me. Her mental state is like overripe tomatoes, leaking and full of slosh. Maybe she has worms."

I snickered at the worm comment, but I couldn't let on that Ruby does make me laugh.

Earl answered Ruby. "She's had a tough patch. I'm not so sure she's dealt with losing her husband and son. She's filled her days with writing and other people's stories, but her story isn't finished or updated. She's lashing out at others with this added grief, and it's more than she can carry."

I shouted, "You know I can hear you!"

Ruby announced, "But can you hear yourself? You're a grown woman sitting in the mud. At least I have enough sense to sit on a curb."

"Go away. I don't need you in my life."

Earl countered, "Maybe you need each other."

Together we reacted, "No, we don't!"

I leaned toward the outer part of the garden on my knees, catching a glimpse of Ruby as she marched to the back porch. She danced and called, "I'll get the labels on the jars. I don't have time to talk to the flowers. Or to hide in the mud and slosh around in self-pity."

I hollered, "I'm not hiding. I'm sitting. Leave me alone."

As the screen to the porch creaked, she added, "Consider it done."

I crossed my legs, and my heart rattled with a thousand high-pitched hammer beats as if my son and husband called to me from beneath the wreckage of the car. I whispered, "God, how do I live life without them? How do I live without my daddy? I can't shut off the horrible memories of my car wreck."

I ached, and my muscles tightened over my bones, suffocation tightened my throat, and every breath I inhaled seemed it might be my last. I closed my eyes, and the flashbacks of seeing Kenny's face when he took a bubble bath swallowed me whole. The short time I had a son, the love inside me grew tenfold. I was like a sweet grape bursting with kindness and sweetness, something many never see in me.

The next flashback sent me to the kitchen in our apartment, where Kyle made coffee with his Keurig and poured cream until the coffee turned a light beige. He always enjoyed a little coffee with his cream, like Daddy.

"I don't want flashbacks of Kyle or Kenny. Or new ones of my daddy. I want them." I sneered, "Where do I belong? It's like I'm not me. I'm no one. I don't fit in the kitchen. At my apartment. And not at a cemetery. I don't belong in this mud either."

I spoke to the sunflower next to me. "Kyle didn't die at the scene on the road. He was alive when I crawled from the car. But when Kyle carried our lifeless Kenny and passed him to my arms, I lost it. I remember rocking and rocking as I sat on the road, clutching my son, watching time stop as my joy shattered into nothingness."

51

I turned back to the okra plants. "I don't know how to act and don't know what to say. The scars of my heart bleed as if the nightmare on the bridge happened yesterday. Kyle, if you loved me, why'd you have to leave? And why did Kenny have to suffer? I can't replace either of you. I want both of you back!"

Standing, the tug of my damp jeans pulled on my legs, and I peeked between the flowers, the large blooms more than six inches across, bright and yellow and bold. I spoke to the sunflower closest to me. "I need someone to breathe life back into me."

Earl cut in, "Sally, your dad's been looking for his daughter to return. He knows you carry your heart in your hands, and life has poured salt into your wounds. So be there for your dad. That will be enough to begin your healing."

I scraped mud from my face. "Earl, have you been listening to me?"

"Yes, as a girl, you always ran to the garden to hide. And Max rescued you from the bumblebees more times than I can count."

"I shouldn't be surprised that you're spying on me. You watch me like a protective parent. Always have." I shuffled between the sunflowers, sighing with relief that I'd left part of my anger behind with the okra plants.

Earl wrapped me in his long arms, accustomed to my fits. "Tell me what the doctor told you. What did he say?"

I licked the dirt from my top lip. *Yuck!* "He told us to prepare to say goodbye. To be ready to make Daddy comfortable." I cried, "He didn't look that sick this morning."

"Don't count your dad out. When you see the stars tonight, remember Max is watching the same sparkle in the sky as you. It might be all right."

I argued, "It might not."

**

In the bathroom, I towel-dried my hair and pulled it into a ponytail. I soaked in the tub for two hours, almost drowning from lack of sleep. Now I'm wearing a fresh shirt, clean pants, and flip-flops. I tossed my mud-caked clothes into the corner with my towel, and my stomach gurgled with an ache. "I haven't eaten all day. I need something now. Maybe a sandwich. And maybe Ruby's gone."

In the living room, Earl held the remote, flipping channels while petting Snowball on the couch. Unfortunately, whenever he stopped clicking, the volume blasted the room. "Earl, turn the TV down. You've got it too loud."

"What? I can't hear you."

"Turn the TV down."

"I'll turn it off. We should get your dad's truck. It's close to six. I need to be home for the news."

"Sure. Where's Ruby?"

"She finished the labels. She slipped out a few minutes ago before you came out of the bathroom. She might be avoiding you."

"The less I see of her, the better. She gets under my skin." I moved to get my purse. "Earl, I don't have Daddy's truck keys. Would he have left them in the cab?"

"Most likely. Max usually leaves them in the ignition."

"Fine, then let's go. And do you mind if I get a cheeseburger from Pitt Grill? I'm starved."

"I could use one too."

As we stepped outside, a cool breeze settled in, but the sky was clear. "Earl, the passenger door is open. Did you get into my car?"

He ran his fingers through his hair. "No, I haven't been to your car or even mine."

I rushed ahead of Earl, pulling the door wide. "No way. Look. My carton of cigarettes is back." I pushed the knob on the glove box. "And look what we have here, the bottle of whiskey has magically returned, too."

"Maybe you've had them the whole time. You have been sitting in mud, crying, and shouting at people. You're distracted and worried about your dad. When a person is upset, life gets muddy."

I shook my head. "Ruby did this. She's returned them to take the heat off. She knows, I know."

"Or you might be mistakenly accusing her."

"I don't think so. Why would the car door be wide open?"

"I don't know. But I tend to believe in people. Years back, I knew you'd kick the alcohol. As for Ruby, she's on the mend, too."

"Wait? Is she bad news for Daddy?"

"No, she's made him smile as he used to when you were … when you were around more."

Earl's words jabbed my heart. "I've been gone too long, haven't I?"

"Yes, some wasted years crept in on you and your dad. Time to make up for things. Time to lift his spirits."

"But what about Ruby? Does she expect to get paid for doing those labels?"

"Yes, and I've paid her. Your dad will repay me with some fried catfish or with ice cream. Or with both."

We climbed into the car, and I backed out of the driveway. "So, where's Ruby now? Is she homeless?"

"She has a few stops she makes. She stays here and there. Sometimes she sleeps on the back porch at your house."

I pulled the car up the road. "My porch? Why would Daddy let her stay with us?"

"Because he cares about people. He thinks kindness shows up in our actions. That's why he gets so many stray cats. He took me in, too, as a friend a hundred years ago. He even paid my rent when I broke my foot and couldn't work before I finished Bible school. They don't come much better than Max."

"You're not a hundred. So does Charcoal belong to Daddy, too?"

"Yes, Snowball and Charcoal. Snowball's laid-back. But that white cat, he's like you, comes with a growl."

"That's not funny. I don't growl."

Earl held his laugh in with his hand. He chuckled, "Really? I'd hate to see you, if you ever did growl."

I nudged his arm. "That's not funny."

"It might be."

"So you think I'm like Charcoal. And Ruby's like Snowball?"

"Watch it; there's a light up there. It's red?"

"I see it." I slowed, asking Earl again, "So do I growl like the cat?"

"You might hiss more than some."

Together we laughed, belly jiggles like old times.

Earl clutched the cigarettes. "Let's toss these in a dumpster. You don't need these."

"I bought the cigarettes on impulse."

"But what about this whiskey? I think we should pour it out too. Trusting God for strength to be brave for your dad won't come by hiding behind a bottle."

"Yes, sir." I held the steering wheel and turned onto Highway 8, driving by the gas station. I twisted my head, staring at the dumpster.

"Who are you looking for? Miss Ruby?"

"Yeah, I ran into her at the Shell gas station last night. That's how she knew me but didn't know me."

"She won't be there. She attends Bible study with Ms. Jeanne on Monday night."

"I didn't take her as a person who studies the Bible."

"Well, she probably has no idea you grew up in church and ran around pews as a girl either."

"I never ran in church."

Earl cleared his throat. "And I never preached a sermon either."

"You preached for a million years at First Baptist, and between you and Daddy, I attended church whenever the doors opened."

Earl nodded. "Those were some great years."

I touched Earl's arm. "I might have run inside the church when I was smaller."

"And then you ran out the door when you got grown."

Ouch! "That's harsh. Like I told Daddy, I grew up."

"But we should grow closer to God, not walk away when life is hard."

I rubbed my ear, unable to debate his response. "It's hard to run to God when you're drowning in a tragedy."

"You can always run to the Lord. The Bible study Ruby attends is for ladies in need of drawing nearer to God."

"I figured you'd throw me in the mix with her. So, what's with that?"

"She could use your friendship. And I think you could use a friend, too."

"Maybe, I'll have to see."

"Ruby's life is involved. Her dad committed suicide when she was ten, and she's struggled to fit in, to find peace with her loss. She ran away from living and hid from most people, sort of like you do. And thankfully, your dad happened upon her."

"What? Happened upon her?"

"Yes, she was eating strawberries one morning from his garden when he caught her."

"So, Daddy gave her a home-cooked meal like biscuits and gravy and eggs?"

"You know your daddy."

"I do. He's the kind of person I hope to grow into someday."

Earl tapped my arm. "What you water is what will grow."

His words wiggled deep into my insides, to the barricaded spot around my heart, where communication to my soul was blocked off with scars. As a retired preacher, Earl tends to fish for lost hearts, and he loves to challenge my faith whenever I'm with him. And boy, have I missed him.

I smiled, "Thank you for being so good to my daddy all these years. And for putting up with me."

"You're welcome. Max has stuck closer to me than a brother. When Minnie died in 2014, he cooked for me. I would have forgotten to eat if Max hadn't watched out for me."

"Daddy's a good one. Do you mind if we eat our burgers inside at Pitt Grill?"

"Let's do it. Then we'll get the truck."

"Sounds good." I pulled into the parking lot next to the hotel.

Earl motioned. "There's Pearson. If you're staying for a while, he's the editor at the newspaper. He could probably use a freelance reporter."

I cut my eyes at Earl, who smirked. I pushed him for an answer. "Did you invite Pearson to meet us?"

"Now would I be sneaky enough to help you find a job?"

I cringed. "Yes, you would."

Pitt Grill Brings Hissing

Inside Pitt Grill, I scooted into a seat next to the window while Earl shuffled into his place across from me. He lined up the catsup behind the salt and pepper shakers and straightened the menus into a perfect stack. He and Daddy have this whole organizing thing down pat, but sometimes in public it's too much.

I shook my head, remembering how Earl ate lunch with us after church almost every Sunday, and how he placed the spoons and forks next to our plates. How he folded napkins, making sure the table aligned with an order. He would line up our glasses to the right of our paper plates, too—everything in its place.

Earl picked up a menu and handed me one. "Let's see what we're having for supper."

I pulled down his menu. "So, you line up the menus, and now it's okay to use them?"

"Yes, starting in order keeps order in place."

Cackling, I asked, "So Pearson's joining us for supper? Is that on the menu too?"

"Maybe, he's talking to someone at the counter, but when he comes over, let's invite him to sit with us."

"He knew we were coming, right?"

"Not necessarily, but since he's here, friends invite friends to eat with them."

"So, they do. But is Pearson going to sit with you on your side?" I snarled, the taste in my mouth salty with sarcasm.

"Pearson doesn't bite. If he sits next to you, being polite is something you should try."

"I'm in no mood to play the polite card. I'm hungry, and that makes me cranky."

"Don't you need a job?"

"You know I do."

"I've prayed for an open door. This could be it."

"You always were a stickler for sharing my life with God."

"When you pray, God does hear you."

Sighing, I kicked Earl under the table. "He's coming over here."

"I thought he might."

"Like I said, where is he going to sit?" I slapped his wrist with my menu, the one touting steaks, waffles, and fine food.

"Stop hitting me. You're not five years old."

"I don't want to meet anyone today. My daddy's sick, and my life's a wreck. And you've given me little Ruby to help. I can't take any more today."

"Sally, don't you think God has your heart in his hands? His mercy is calling to you. Walk where He guides. And remember, God often interrupts our day to draw us closer to Him."

"Now you're stepping on my toes, big time. I'm leaving."

Earl wrapped his fingers around my hands. "I'll sit by you. Slide over."

"Thank you." I hung next to the window, peering out the pane, hoping to ignore Pearson, who shadowed our table.

Pearson greeted us. "Hello, Earl. So, is this my new freelancer?"

I borrowed a smile from the lady at the following table, biting my bottom lip before answering. "Hi, I'm Sally."

Earl nodded. "She's a great storyteller and writer."

"So I've heard." Pearson added, "It's been a long time."

"A long time from …"

59

"Since we've seen each other."

I didn't play along and hated the idea that we knew each other, but politely answered, "Yes, it has. But unfortunately, life tends to take us down roads that often bring us back home."

Pearson held his menu, looking over it. "A detour can often be the right path."

"Oh my, more counseling from the cheap seats."

Earl cleared his throat. "Sally Snow. Manners are welcome here."

"Sorry, Pearson. I'm a little touchy today."

"No problem. Hey, you should work for me. I've heard you have experience."

I threw darts with my eyes, ready to mouth about how he knew such a thing, but Earl interrupted my wave of one-liners. "Pearson, we're about to order burgers. We're starving."

Pearson nodded. "Yes, some people get grouchy if they're hungry. Or so I've heard."

I tried not to smile, but my lips rebelled against my will. I piped in, "I'm getting scrambled eggs with cheese, hash browns, and crispy bacon. Maybe two pieces of sausage and toast." My ramblings ended with me looking down at the menu. "I think I'll order two waffles too, with bananas on top."

Earl nudged me. "You barely weigh a hundred pounds; where will you put that much food?"

I raised my eyebrows, offering a juicy response as if syrup dripped from the dispenser over my attitude. "I've not eaten for hours. I'm way past starving." I turned to Pearson. "And by the way, I'm capable of finding a job. Thank you very much."

Pearson put his menu down, one leg in the booth and the other outside. "Maybe this is a bad idea for me to eat with you, but I need a good reporter. One who can prove herself by covering Pioneer Days with photos and a feature story. That person might find herself in a full-time position. Pay's not great. But if she loves writing, she'll have plenty to write about in the county."

Earl stacked my menu with his and took Pearson's from his grip. "We're all hungry. A meal will be good for all of us." He then passed the menus out in an orderly fashion, again, as if we hadn't held them seconds before my sarcastic outbursts. Earl glanced my way, giving me that same eye-piercing stare he used to from the pulpit when I wiggled too much in church as a girl.

I sat up straight. "I'm sorry for my rudeness. But unfortunately, it comes easier these days to run people off."

Pearson covered his mouth as if trying to keep a smile from landing in our midst. Instead, he muttered, "I've had a long day myself. Someone mailed me a letter telling me I'm biased at the paper. Whoever it was didn't like a story I wrote. I gave it my twist, but someone disagreed with the approach. So the letter showed up and ruined my day."

Earl changed the subject. "I buy the paper for the crossword puzzle."

Pearson laughed. "Well, at least you don't think the puzzle's biased."

"Maybe I do. Maybe I should write an anonymous letter to you."

Pearson picked up where he left off. "That person didn't put their name on the letter, so I can't even respond to it. I've fumed about it all day. I missed lunch, and I knocked over a plant from a shelf and broke the pot. Finally, everyone at the office decided to leave early. I'm sure I was too loud. But I was mad."

Earl pointed to Pearson's menu. "Food. We all need food."

I slumped down in the seat. "I'm sorry. I had no right to speak to you with my bitter tone. Let's start over. I need food too. And apparently, I'll need dessert. Because dessert makes me happy."

Pearson shuffled into the seat; his buttoned shirt was ironed, fresh from the cleaners. "I'm off to cover a school board meeting tonight. A meal will help me endure the night."

Earl jumped right on Pearson's statement. "You work too many hours."

"Yeah, we're a bit short-handed. I've lost two reporters in the past five years. They move on to other adventures."

I shook my head, the conversation moving right back to where we'd left off. I sensed my rudeness rushing up my neck like a contagious rash. I was about to show out again. I took in the deepest breath, counting to ten. I didn't want to remind Earl that I'm a cat with claws.

The waitress stepped to our table after pouring coffee at the counter and greeted us with too many questions. "What are we drinking today? Tea? Cokes? Or freshly brewed coffee?"

I sighed, not sure if drinking coffee with the summer's heat made sense. "I'd like ice-cold water with a lemon slice on the rim."

She chuckled, "If I pour water on ice, it's cold. As for the lemon, we're out of lemons."

"Seriously, no lemons?" That invisible rash returned, raced up to my ears, but I pushed it deep inside, keeping my lousy attitude at bay. I didn't want to release it on another unsuspecting soul. I touched my throat. "I'm sorry. That's perfectly fine."

Earl smiled, almost as if he were a proud father of a girl who showed a teeny bit of self-control. He patted my leg as if he approved of my one shining moment, and I caught myself laughing behind my menu.

Pearson cocked his head to my left, which was his right. "I can't decide between breakfast food or a cheeseburger and fries."

I licked my lips. "Thanks, now I want a cheeseburger."

Pearson tapped the table like he was using a typewriter and writing a story. "Let's see. Breakfast? Or cheeseburger? What to get?"

I chimed in. "Now, don't be biased to the cheeseburger. You might get an anonymous letter about it."

Earl snickered, as I did, and Pearson cracked up, pounding the table with his fist. "That's not funny." He paused, "Okay, so it was funny. That's a good one, Sunflower."

"Wait, you called me Sunflower."

"Well, I'm sorry. Are you too grown up for that now? It's what I called you in high school when we were on the debate team."

"We were never on the debate team together."

"We were. That class was extra credit for first-year students, and you were the top-achieving type, so you had to do it all. You were trying to outshine the others."

"I don't remember that class."

"You should. You yelled a lot."

Another tap stopped the chatter, and the waitress joined in with her debate. "Excuse me. Let me get your drinks. Earl, you're going to want tea, right? And Pearson, is it Diet Coke or real Coke?"

Pearson looked up at the giant woman, whose face shone as if she could use some face powder and a bit of lipstick. He announced, "I'll take a real Coke today."

"What is a real Coke?" I hounded him as if we were back in debate class.

"It's a soda with sugar."

"So, a Diet Coke isn't real?"

Earl piped in, "Both of you, stop this. I can't focus on what to order."

The waitress huffed away, and Pearson gave me a wink, not a flirty wink, just the kind of friend might provide you when you're trying to annoy a retired preacher. We placed our order a few minutes later, and the table became covered with plates of cheeseburgers for Earl and Pearson and my array of breakfast foods. Unfortunately, Earl couldn't rearrange the plates straight because there wasn't room to line them up.

By the time I dabbed up the last bit of waffles and bacon, Earl had downed his cheeseburger, followed by a scoop of ice cream; Pearson stood to say his goodbyes. "Sally, I've enjoyed interviewing you for the job at the paper. It's yours if you want it. Let me know by the end of the week." He turned to Earl. "I've got this. My treat."

I held my fork in the air, pointing at him. "You didn't interview me, and I never asked for a job."

Earl wiped his mouth with his napkin. "Sally, take the job. You need the money. He needs help. And you love writing."

As I considered changing my mind, a man charged into the restaurant. "Call for help. Someone just hit the sign out front. A woman's on the ground. She's unconscious."

I got on my knees and stood on the seat in the booth, the sun barely peeking over the gas station across the road, the night settling on us. "Earl, is that Daddy's truck? And is that, Ruby?"

We charged from the restaurant, racing like we were on a track team, each of us hoping to get to the finish line first. Earl's long legs outpaced Pearson's and mine. He turned Ruby from her side, and he whispered to her limp body. "Poor girl, what happened?"

64

A screaming, out-of-control woman climbed from a parked white car. "Why did I let her drive? What was I thinking?"

Earl rushed to the short-haired woman whose pants and shirt matched, whose hair was brown like her clothes. She wailed, "This is my fault. I'll never forgive myself."

Pearson rushed to his truck, returning with a camera while I twirled around, taking in the commotion. He handed me the camera. I barked, "Wait, this isn't the kind of story this town needs. What are you thinking?"

"It's news. This is your first assignment."

"But no ... I'm not covering this accident."

Pearson stepped around me. "Fine." He took the camera from me. "I'm taking a photo of the truck that's mangled with the Pitt Grill sign. I won't divulge any facts or release anything until I know I can."

"You better not. Or I won't come to work for you." I surprised myself, offering up a bit of integrity in the middle of the chaos.

Earl now held his arms around the hysterical woman as they stood by her car. Another couple of people knelt next to Ruby. Finally, Earl put me to work. "Stay with Jeanne. She holds the Bible study at the church, and she gave Ruby a ride to get Max's pickup."

The mascara-laced cheeks of the woman, along with her erratic shaking, sent me to my wreck from two years ago, to a place I never want to go. The desire to help Ruby dominated my thoughts more than my renewed sorrow. I held a napkin in my hand from the restaurant. "Here, wipe off your face. I'm sure Ruby's going to be fine." I peered across the parking lot, unable to know that what I said was true.

Jeanne cried, "I don't know what happened. I was behind her, and she lost control, and the truck weaved between a diesel and a pack of cars. It's a wonder she didn't cause the other cars to crash into each other."

"She just left the road? Does she have a driver's license?" Unfortunately, my second question was out of line and out of my mouth before I could retrieve it.

Sniffling, Jeanne coughed. "She may be homeless. But she can drive."

"I'm sorry. I shouldn't have asked such a thing. But Ruby must have had trouble with the truck for it to run off the highway."

"Yes, something was going on, and she even slowed down. She was waving her arms in the cab right before the crash." Jeanne wiped snot from her nose with the back of her hand. "This is my fault. What was I thinking?"

Weeblewooo. Weeblewooo.

An ambulance pulled next to Ruby, where the waitress from our meal now knelt, and she prayed for Ruby, and the men wearing caps took off their caps as if to show respect.

"Dear God, bring Ruby through this. Heal her body. Let the doctors know how to help her. Amen."

I noticed she said Ruby's name, and I figured the waitress had given Ruby food from the kitchen sometimes.

The same two EMTs from this morning, a bouncy woman and a loping man, each gave me a second glance as they rushed to Ruby's side. I hoped they didn't think I had anything to do with Daddy's incident and now this one.

I wiped a lone tear and ran to Earl's side. "I bring bad luck. Look at this. Daddy's in the hospital, and now Ruby's hurt."

"You don't have that kind of power, my sweet girl. Stand with Jeanne. Her husband, Ricky, is coming to comfort her and to take her home."

"Yes, sir." I obeyed, not sure what standing with a crying woman could do to help the situation.

As we waited, as the police circled in and left, and as the ambulance loaded Ruby onto the stretcher, a tow truck backed up to get Daddy's truck off the premises, and Ricky took Jeanne home.

I asked Earl, "Where will they tow Daddy's truck?"

"I'm not sure. I'll find out."

Earl tapped on the man's shoulder, whose greasy pants held oil and dirt from other jobs. But before Earl could ask, the man flew backward. "Oh, my word!"

I caught myself jumping with the man, not sure why.

He bounced back another ten feet, pushing Earl to the side. The man hollered, "I don't do rattlesnakes. I'm not moving this truck until that thing is dead!"

Pam Kumpe

Rattlesnake Friends

After a tense evening of watching more than a dozen men in jeans and T-shirts do the hokey pokey around one little snake, along with volunteer firefighters who joined the search, who didn't dance any better, I was worn out.

If Daddy had found the snake, he would have taken the horrible thing to the woods and let it go. So, I'm proud Daddy is resting at the hospital and not anywhere near his truck.

The rattlesnake remained curled up beneath the seat, and after about thirty minutes, and after too many folks jabbed at him with sticks, the snake was back under the seat. I'll have nightmares tonight, and the heebie-jeebies and creepy crawler tingles are already pricking my skin.

At one point, an overweight man tripped and fell over two regular-sized men, and the three of them came up swinging, then running off and hiding behind a fire truck. I'm sure the rattlesnake enjoyed their show as much as I did.

As for hungry patrons, the manager at the Pitt Grill closed the restaurant during the commotion because his parking lot had become a circus of actors, most of whom did not know their role in the ring. Or how to trap a wild snake.

Eventually, Pearson left for his meeting but passed his Canon on to me, asking me to take photos. I've taken plenty of photographs before, but tonight, many of my shots are blurred, except for one picture of those three men, arms out, faces red, eyes bulging with fear. They will thank me for deleting the image from the camera card.

After three hours, Earl advised everyone to settle down, to go home, and that he would return with his shotgun. Now, a preacher carrying a gun to shoot a snake is what I should have taken photos of, but Earl might have tossed Pearson's camera into the trash if I'd pointed the lens at him.

When Earl returned, dressed for the part, wearing his straw hat and overalls, he stomped in heavy boots on a mission, holding his gun like a warrior. The firefighter closest to him advised Earl that shooting in the city limits would not be tolerated. But Earl took that as a suggestion and aimed.

Earl told him, "You'd best send folks home. I'll get this snake with one shot. The snake needs calm and needs quiet; then he'll show his head."

One by one, the looky-loos went home, and soon it was just Earl and me and one firefighter. The windows on the truck were down, which is how we assumed the snake got into the cab in the first place.

I waited in my car, tapping the steering wheel with my fingers, with my windows up. Snakes are not my friend. Once, a four-foot black snake almost took my life in high school. The blue jays were squawking and stirring up a commotion around the branches. I thought maybe a bird's nest was under attack, so I hurried beneath the tree, gazing up. To my surprise, a snake flopped from the tree onto my feet.

That day, I found myself on the back porch, hiding behind the screen door. I hollered for Daddy, and he moved outside with a hoe to push the snake into a trash can, then placed a lid over the top and let the black monster loose in the woods right behind our house.

I remember telling Daddy all snakes should die, and he quickly reminded me not to be in such a hurry to kill something.

Well, Earl must have learned snake-hunting and corralling them from Daddy. His tactics were hilarious, plenty of sneaking and pausing and waiting for the snake to slither an inch or to show its head. Earl would agree with me, in this case, a rattlesnake in Daddy's truck must die.

He lingered with his gun as if holding an altar call, like preachers do when they wait to see if someone is ready to make a profession of faith. I hoped the snake was ready to make a profession by exiting the truck.

Earl yelled, "I see him. He's on the dash."

I heard the affirming shouts inside my car, so much for quietness and a calm approach. Instead, Earl's voice came to life, as if he were teaching from Genesis and discussing the snake's deception. "Make your move, you silly snake."

I chuckled, thankful Earl never spoke to his congregation like he did that snake. If he had held church altar calls with words like, "Make your move, you filthy sinner," I'm sure the people would have let him go.

In a few minutes, the snake slithered from one side of the dashboard to the other, wrapping himself around the steering wheel, methodically twisting and bending into a coil, only to unwrap with a jerk, and straighten out as he slithered out the open driver's seat window.

I cringed, knowing Earl was a good shot, but he stepped too close, and it was as if the snake made eye contact with Earl, and my heart pounded like a drumbeat. I cracked my door open. "Earl, be careful. Back up!"

Earl bent his head toward me. "Hush, get inside the car."

I slammed the door, watching and holding my breath, and I found myself praying, "Lord, that's Earl. You know him. Don't let him miss. Daddy needs Earl. Everyone needs Earl."

The salty taste of East Texas sweat poured over me as a river exploded on top of my head, but the sweat wasn't horrible like hairspray tonight.

Kaboom!

Almost in slow motion, the rattlesnake crumpled to the ground like a broken rubber band, his rattler flinching with movement, but his head no longer existed at the other end.

I shot from the car like a bullet. "You did it! You got the snake. You're the best shot in town."

I was shaking like a thousand bumblebees were waiting to sting my neck.

Earl held his gun to his side. "I'm thankful that the first shot hit him. I only had one bullet."

"What? You brought one bullet?"

"I only needed one if the snake cooperated."

"Well, I'm glad to know he was obedient."

The applause from the few lingering people meant they'd go home, and we'd have Daddy's truck towed. And Pitt Grill would reopen for late meals. After all, the lights still flickered with the invitation to eat at the cafe, even though the pole hung in half, over to the side.

The door to the restaurant swung open, and our waitress from earlier, who was inside watching the whole incident, waved for me to come over to her. I yelled, "What do you want? We're good. We're not hungry."

"I need one of you to pay your bill. Pearson had it but left with the ticket. Can you or Earl take care of this?"

I sauntered over to Earl, who hovered over the snake as if he'd slaughtered a mountain lion in the mountains of Montana. He nudged me. "That's the biggest snake I've seen in this part of town in years."

"Nice. It's dead, right?" I backed up, the sweat in my eyes ripping away the outer layer of my corneas.

"The snake is dead. See, no head."

"Can you put the thing in a sack or something? I can't stand looking at the snake."

Earl motioned to the firefighter. "Hey, do you have a trash bag?"

Ms. Waitress, whose face shone in the shadow of the Monday sunset, whose face was oilier than during our meal, announced, "I'll give you a trash bag if you pay for your meal."

Earl nodded. "Consider it done."

**

After our meal was paid for, the truck was towed, and Earl took Jeanne her car with me following, I dropped Earl off at his house so he could put away his snake hat and gun. Back inside my living room, Earl phoned the hospital and planned for me to pick up Ruby.

I rubbed my eyes. "You're determined to put Ruby and me together, aren't you?"

"I'm living out my faith."

"Whatever! You're trying to put order in my life."

Earl nodded. "I like serving God and being His vessel."

"I bet God could have used you and your gun in the Garden of Eden."

"No, Adam and Eve never had access to guns back then, and I wouldn't have interfered with God's plan for redeeming the hearts of mankind."

"Goodness, you go from snake killer to preacher mode in one sentence."

"I've preached many sermons through the years; it's in my blood."

"You're right about that; I'll go see Daddy and get Ruby."

In my car, I relished how Earl loved setting things right in the world. But if I don't get some sleep, I'm going to fall over.

I hope Ruby knows I'm coming to take her to Daddy's house, something I never expected to be doing. Something I'm going to regret, I'm sure.

Three Stars

I parked close to the awning at the main entrance of the hospital, and the dashboard clock showed it was close to ten. No wonder I had plenty of places to park; visiting hours had ended. I announced to anyone within range as I hopped from the car, "I'm stopping by Daddy's room first before I find Ruby."

At the end of the hall, I took the elevator and pushed the button for Daddy's floor, ready to rush to his side. I tried the door to his room and marched inside, whispering, "Daddy, it's me." I got closer to his face. "Daddy, are you awake?"

"Awake? Who can sleep in this place? Every few minutes, someone takes my blood pressure or checks my temperature. Or fixing my IV."

"What's in the IV?"

"You'll have to ask the nurse. I've forgotten."

"How are you feeling, better?"

"I'm good right now. Did you know the doctor touches his right eyebrow whenever he gives me bad news?"

"Is that true?"

"Yes, he's done the eyebrow thing every time I see him."

"Maybe he has a tick, and he does it when he shares good news, too."

"Okay, I'll take that for now. But this morning, the humidity got me, that's all." He patted the mattress and smiled. "Sit by me. Earl phoned and told me what happened with Ruby and a rattlesnake and with my truck."

I touched his arm. "Do you let Ruby drive your truck?"

"She doesn't have a vehicle, so yes. If she's making jam deliveries for me, it's helpful for her to have a way to tote the crates."

"But how would she know that you left the keys in the ignition?" I prodded as if I held a needle, pressing for answers.

"I leave my keys in the truck at the house, too. No one would take that old thing." Daddy squinted. "Ruby's kind to me and helpful. Stop looking for a reason to get rid of her."

"I'll try. But now you'll need a new ride since Ruby wrecked your truck."

"The snake is the culprit, not Ruby. Besides, there's a black pickup at the dealership I've admired for months. We'll have to go look at it."

"Yes, we'll get you something you like. Maybe you should be the only one driving it, though," I hinted, hugging his neck. "Well, I'd better go find Ruby."

"You'd better take care of Ruby and treat her like I treat you. As for who drives my truck, I'll make the decision."

"Yes, sir," I conceded.

"Earl told me how you sat in the garden today when you had a panic attack."

"It wasn't a panic attack. When I go to the garden, the noise inside my head goes away."

"But you're a grown woman. Sitting in the mud and crying isn't healthy."

"So, you think I'm a bad example for your sunflowers?" I nestled up to hug his neck again. "I'll work on being kind and putting up with Ruby. But the garden is like a clubhouse for me."

"Clubhouses are safe havens and usually in a tree. But children grow up. It's time to stand tall like a sunflower."

"Oh, Daddy, when I'm with you, I want to be five again."

"You'll always be my girl, but you are approaching forty."

"I'll be thirty-nine in January. Don't make me older than I am."

Daddy put his hand under my chin. "Always be kind. The purpose is to make others feel welcome. And don't run Ruby off."

"Yes, sir." I nestled on the mattress next to Daddy. "But when I go to the garden, I can let all my brokenness go. And when I'm there, it's like you are with me."

"Sunflower, when you rely on God, you are safe. So, dare to believe even when your path is long and slow. Let God be your guide."

"Yes, Daddy, but I'm full of doubts."

"Your detours have brought you home, and the new path is ahead. Be patient, keep watch. See what blooms. Be ready for a rescue of the heart."

"The last two years have tested my faith. But God knows what's best for me, even if I cry, or shout, or whenever I do both."

Daddy pushed the button on his bed, raising his head, sitting higher up. "You've got a lot of questions. Take life, one day at a time."

"You always believe in people. And I've let you down. I never planned for my drinking to control me. Rehab wasn't on my radar."

"But you did the work and found your way. Cancer wasn't on my radar either, but with God, I'll run my race and finish well."

"Earl talked about running to God today, too. So, it seems I should take your advice and his."

"Just don't leave the window down on your heart, or a snake might slither up and bite you."

"Daddy, I'll be kind to Ruby if she doesn't pester me."

"She probably pesters you because you're an easy target. Give her a reason to trust you, and she will. Oh, and let her know I appreciate her putting the labels on the jars." He pushed the button on the bed, kissing my cheek. "I'd forgotten I asked her to do them. You got your feelings hurt, didn't you?"

"I might have. We fought like kids today."

"Yes, Earl told me that part too."

I giggled. "Does Earl tell you everything?"

"He does if I need to know. Now run on, I'll be home soon. And tell Ruby that I love her."

My heart ripped into a million pieces inside my chest. "Did you say you love Ruby?"

"I do love her, like a new daughter in the family. She's about your age. And I've enjoyed her company." Daddy held me close. "Don't worry, you've got the special spot in my heart, and no one can replace you. You're my baby girl."

I sighed, "I love you, Daddy. I'm sorry for being so sensitive."

"You're like your mother. She was sensitive too. You would have loved her."

"You've told me all my life how special she was to you."

"She was ... she still is. I'm glad we were together for your mother's birthday earlier."

"Me, too. And you sang to her."

"Yes, but don't tell Earl. He'll make fun of me."

"Earl's one to talk. He can't carry a tune."

I jumped from the bed. "Well, I'm supposed to meet Ruby in the lobby, and here I am with you. I'd better go; the hospital has probably discharged her."

Daddy kissed the top of my red mop. "Make me proud. Dig deep. You have Williams' genes. And those are good genes. Don't forget."

"Yes, sir. I understand. I'll behave."

As I stepped out of the elevator onto the first floor after saying goodnight to Daddy, I thought about Ruby and how scared she must have been driving a truck with a snake. I would have flat-out died if I'd gotten that close to a snake.

I passed a window by the winding hallway which led to the main entrance, and I glanced up at the night sky, where three stars sparkled at me. "So, God, are you showing me that Daddy, Ruby, and I belong together? If so, you could have done it without using a snake."

Rounding the hallway, I marched into the lobby where an attendant stood behind a wheelchair, and the woman faced the other way. I got even with them and recognized Ruby, who had a bandage on her head. "I'm sorry, did you wait long?"

The young man in scrubs turned and responded, "No, only a second or two, I'll bring her out to your car."

Ruby's head was wrapped in gauze, her face held stitches on her left cheek, and there were places on her arms that looked like the pavement tried to skin her. I used nice words. "I'll get the car. I bet you're hungry."

Ruby shot back. "We've been here ten minutes. You were supposed to meet me here. And look, you're wandering around and making me wait. I asked for a few minutes to see Max, but no, I'm stuck in this wheelchair waiting for you."

"Well, I'm glad to see the accident didn't change your pleasant personality."

Ruby reached for her head. "Can we go? I'm worn thin. My patience is too."

"My car's outside. I'll pull it under the awning."

**

As we moved onto the interstate, sitting beside each other in the car, I shook my head at the irony of having Ruby with me. I couldn't believe she was sleeping at the house tonight, too. In the past 24 hours, so much has changed, so much is the same, yet in many ways it is different. A load of anger got dumped in the mud today when I sat with the sunflowers. No one understands how unique my daddy's garden is to me. And now, I've picked up another load, and she talks too much and makes me spout off things I wish I could take back.

I peeked over at Ruby, wondering if she had stolen my cigarettes and whiskey or if she was telling the truth about someone else getting into my car. But it didn't make sense; why wouldn't the thief take my purse or backpack? And who would return stolen items later?

Ruby interrupted my thoughts. "Whatever is on the floor is in my way." She bent over, picking up the cigarettes and the bottle. "So, when did these show up?"

"You tell me?"

"I have no idea. But you accused me of stealing them."

"Toss them in the back seat. I'm throwing them out when we get home. Earl thinks I should rid myself of things that add to my sorrow."

"I have to agree with Earl; he's full of wise words."

For a second, I almost mentioned how getting rid of her might help, but instead, I swallowed my words. Remembering what Daddy said about leaving a window down on my heart, I knew a snake of hatred had slithered inside. I mouthed to the invisible snake. "I've got to shut those windows."

Ruby glanced around. "The windows are up."

"Yeah, so they are."

Ruby rubbed her stomach. "I could use something to eat if you don't mind."

"We'll stop at Wendy's when we get off the interstate. I'm sure they're open all night." I blurted out one more question.

"So, tell the truth, did you return my things after I called you on it?"

"Seriously. Let this go. And no, I never had them in the first place."

"Right, so not one person knows I'm asking about my cigs and bottle of whiskey except you, and they suddenly show up after our argument."

Ruby sighed, "Do you have air conditioning? It's like a sauna."

"It's hot because you know you took my things."

"I'm burning up because there's no cool air anywhere in this car."

"Tell the truth. Did you return the cigarettes and whiskey?"

"If I tell you, will you turn me over to the police?"

I coughed, caught off guard. Was she about to fess up? I thought about what Daddy would say and not what I'd say. "Fine. Just tell me. I won't call the police."

"I did get in your car for my hoodie. After you were annoying and in my face, I checked out your car. It's a moment I regret. I took the carton of cigarettes, and I hit the button on the glove box with my elbow. It opened, and the bottle was there for the taking."

My lips pursed, and I wanted to scream, but the three stars in the sky were the size of the moon, reminding me of Daddy's love for Ruby and his love for me. "So, do you steal from my daddy?"

"Never. Not once. I promise. Last night I was stuck in the past and hiding from my life." She put her hand to her mouth. "Sorry, let's just say I wasn't myself last night. I'd had a horrible afternoon."

My sandpaper responses churned inside my head, and I longed to follow Daddy's advice, hoping to offer genuine concern. "I'm sorry. I've had a rough two years. I've been stuck for a long time, too."

Ruby wiped her face. "I sometimes wish I could become invisible and could hide forever."

A place in my heart opened to her words. "Ruby, you already know my life's a mess. And harder than I wish. I hid in the garden in the mud today, for heaven's sake. But I have no right to judge you. I might have drunk the whiskey or smoked a cigarette if you hadn't taken them. I'm struggling these days."

"I can't seem to give up the cigarettes. But that was my last pack." She looked down at the carton. "We've got to get rid of these things. They're stumbling blocks for us."

"Yes, the first dumpster I see, in they go."

Ruby placed them back on the floor. "I've learned a new scripture in Bible study. Can I share it with you?"

"So did Earl or Daddy put you up to this?"

"Up to what?"

"To preach to me."

"It's a verse. I thought you might like something to encourage you. You don't have to be so testy."

"Sorry, tell me the verse." I turned on the blinker and steered the car right, taking the exit. "Honestly, I'm thankful the snake didn't bite you."

"He missed me when I got thrown from the truck." Ruby rocked in her seat. "Did you change the subject so I wouldn't share the verse?"

I shrugged my shoulders. "Maybe I have trouble focusing."

"No kidding." Ruby put her hand to her chin. "It goes like this: Fear not, I am with you. Don't be dismayed because I am your God. I will strengthen you and help you. And I will

81

uphold you with my righteous right hand. Those verses are from Isaiah 41, I think."

"Okay, thanks."

"Don't you love it? God is our strength. He holds us, which takes the pressure off us. We can stop being afraid because He's got us."

"Okay, it's a good verse."

"You are hard to talk to."

"I'm a tough case, or so I've heard."

I turned the car to the right at the light, then left for Wendy's, right past Pitt Grill. "What do you want? They have a drive-thru window."

"I'd like a cheeseburger with mustard. And a real Coke."

"What's with you people? A Coke is real. Just say Coke."

"See, you are testy."

"And worn out. Sorry." I made the circle to the window, and we picked up our order, which put us right across from Pitt Grill. I stopped at the road before pulling out. "Did I tell you that Earl shot the snake with one bullet?"

"No, but I've heard he's a good shot."

I yawned. "I can't wait to get some sleep. I'm so tired."

Ruby took a bite of her burger, mumbling her words with food in her mouth. "Tired? I'm the one with a concussion. And you don't have stitches in your face."

"What do you want me to say? I'm not happy you're hurt, but not all scars are on the outside." I swallowed hard, trying not to argue with her.

"Sorry. I'm tired too." Ruby held her real Coke and gobbled down her burger, and I noticed her shredded clothes, probably from landing on the asphalt.

Once in the driveway, I offered to let Ruby sleep in Daddy's bed. She shook her head. "No, thank you. The cot on the porch is good enough. I'll stay there. I'll feed the cats first. I'm sure they're hungry. *"*

Meow. Meow.

Charcoal and Snowball met us in the yard, prancing like starving and lonely kitties. As I petted Snowball, Charcoal rubbed up against my leg. "Well, you've decided to be friendly."

Ruby grabbed up the white ball of fluff. "He's not hard to love once you get to know him."

I held Snowball close. "I guess we're all a little hard to love at first." I stopped in the yard beside one of the Mimosa trees. "Who's on the porch?"

"I'm not sure."

The shadow pounced in front of us, and the cats tumbled from our grasp, dashing around the house. The man asked, "Ruby, where have you been? We need to talk."

Pam Kumpe

Runaway Now

Ruby put herself between the bushy-faced bear-of-a-man and me, and then, looking over her shoulder, she motioned for me to wait. She edged up to the shadow, lowering her voice. "Meet me later. We'll talk then."

"It's later now. Besides, you didn't show up at the gas station, and the police and fire trucks went by around sundown—too many cops around for me. I ended up sitting by the statue at the courthouse, and I moved on and walked here. I've been playing with the cats."

"The officers and fire trucks were coming to my accident."

"You had an accident? Doing what?"

"I was driving a pickup, and there was a rattlesnake in the cab."

"Sure you were, and I have a brand-new Jeep at the car dealer, and I'm picking it up tomorrow."

Ruby pushed him like a sister might, hard but playful. "Seriously, I had Max's truck. There was a snake inside, and I lost control when it got on the seat."

I wiped my bangs from my eyes and folded my arms, my feet aching to get in the middle of their conversation. I stomped up next to them. "What in the world is this all about? I take it you two are friends?"

The hooded man with the scraggly beard asked, "And you are?"

I spouted back. "I should be asking you that question. This is my daddy's house. You're on my porch. And you're the one trespassing."

Ruby pulled my arm, yanking my body like I was spaghetti being tossed by a fork. "Use your inside voice."

I turned to her. "I have a right to know who's on the porch. And since you're staying here until your head's better, we don't need any surprises. Who is he?"

The not-my-friend inched closer, and he grabbed Ruby's arm. "You need to come with me. I need some advice."

Ruby ushered him away. "I'll meet you behind the house by the garden. Let me go inside with Sally and let me convince her you're not here to rob her or anything."

I wiggled up to Ruby. "Once again, you're talking as if I can't hear you. Tell me who this man is and why he thinks you should stand outside with him at this late hour."

Ruby wiped her face, grimacing when she touched her stitches. *Ouch!* "He's my … my brother. We meet on Monday nights at the gas station. We're trying to stay in touch."

I shook my head, knowing her explanation didn't ring true. "So, if he's your brother, wouldn't he care that there's a giant wad of gauze wrapped around your head? Wouldn't he ask about the stitches on your face? And wouldn't he want to know if the snake bit you? Or why your clothes are mangled like shredded lettuce?"

The nighttime-surprise rubbed his beard. "Ruby, I'm gone. We're going to talk. You have to help me."

Ruby sighed, "Sorry, I didn't plan to crash the truck and get hurt."

I ushered Ruby to the door. "Come inside."

"You don't have to push."

"If I were pushing you, you would know it." I peeked out the front door, gazing into the yard, and pushed the screen open wider, stretching my neck. I looked back at Ruby. "Do I need to phone Earl?"

Ruby bumped into the coffee table. "Shut the door. He's not going to break into the house or come for you. He simply wants to talk to me."

I slammed the door, turned the lock, and leaned against the door, my questions dropping like a cat clawing for answers. "Are you in trouble? Who is he? He's not your brother. I don't want you getting my daddy mixed up in illegal stuff. Who meets a person at night at a gas station? That's not normal."

"Like you're normal? Remember, you're the one who sat in the mud talking to plants today, and you're the one who shouts at dumpsters. And don't forget, you met me at a gas station."

I stewed, circling Ruby, unsure of my next argument. "Three days ago, when Earl's letter came, you were not in my plan."

"You weren't in mine either. I was fine before you showed up."

"You were fine only because you're trying to get in good with my daddy."

Ruby countered, "Are you taking me down that road again? As for your daddy, he's not that old."

"Well, I didn't come home to see you. I came for my daddy. And look, you're making trouble, and now I'm babysitting you."

"Nothing crazy happened until you drove home. You can pack and leave if you like. No one will mind."

Her tone cut like a steak knife, slicing at my heart. "My daddy will mind."

"Yeah, and he'll get on with life when you get on with yours."

Bang. Bang. Bang.

We spun around toward the pounding on the front door, which stopped our arguing, and we glared at each other as if we might not answer it.

I whispered, "So much for making this work."

A blur of words filtered from the other side of the door. "Hey, what's the commotion? Someone open this door."

I inched toward the door. "Who's there?"

"It's Earl. Ruby and Sally, open this door. I know you can hear me."

I turned to Ruby. "Wonderful, now Earl's here."

Ruby stomped on the paper airplanes beside the chair. "This is your fault. And stop accusing me of causing problems. You're the problem."

"You're determined to make me mad. Tell the truth, is that guy waiting for you by the sunflowers, your brother?"

"No, but did you think the front yard, in the dark, late at night, around midnight, is a great time to explore this topic? My friend gets bossy, like you. I could just imagine how you two might argue."

I twisted the knob, opening the door. "I'm not bossy. I have a lot to say."

Earl bounced inside as if his legs were numb, his stance awkward. He wiped his eyes, standing in Pac-Man PJs. "What are you two shouting about? I woke up to Snowball and Charcoal hissing and spitting outside my bedroom window, only to hear you two hissing and spitting like you're fighting for territorial rights."

I snickered, drooling on my hand. "Earl, do you know that your pajamas have Pac-Man on them?"

"I grew up playing that video game. Max gave them to me for Christmas a few years ago as a joke. But they're my favorite." He paused. "Don't change the subject. This is ridiculous. Am I going to have to babysit both of you?"

Ruby sauntered up to Earl like a cat does when they make up with you. "Sally's unreasonable. She barks at me as if I'm her puppet. And she's ready to accuse me of things imagined in her mind." She touched her head. "I need to sit down. My brain is shooting fireworks behind my ears."

Earl hugged her with one arm. "Over here, sit down. You've gone through so much today." In his preacher's voice, he growled at me. "And you, sit down at the other end. I'm surrounded by two women who are acting like children."

I plopped down and kicked a paper airplane, which skidded sideways, its wings bent. I sighed. "I was about to call you. We're not safe. A man was sitting on our porch when we got here. He's after Ruby."

Ruby tucked her feet beneath her and put her head on a pillow. "He's not after me." She closed her eyes, almost as fast as those words settled in the room.

Earl put his finger to his lips. *Shh!* "She's exhausted. Poor thing." He reached for the black-and-white velour blanket draped over the back of the recliner, the one I sent to Daddy for his birthday.

I hid my tears behind my hands, wiping my face. My whines leaked from my lips as he covered Ruby with the blanket. "Earl, I'm pretty tired too."

"Tiredness is no excuse for not showing hospitality."

I rolled into a ball on my end of the couch, and Ruby's legs took up more than half of the cushions. "Earl, please, it's too late for one of your sermons."

Earl moved to the door, twisting the lock, and sat in Daddy's recliner, lifting the handle and raising his feet, those wearing Pac Man slippers.

I chuckled, "I guess Daddy bought those for you, too."

"No, I found these on the clearance aisle at Walmart."

I settled into my spot, taking a glance at the clock on the wall, a reminder that I had not slept many hours in the last two days.

Earl tapped his finger on the arm of his chair. "You're sleepy, I can see that, so this will be short."

I rolled my eyes, knowing that's like Earl saying, 'as I continue to close,' and not doing so, while preaching.

Earl went on, tapping two fingers on his chair. "Sally, in Proverbs 14, it says that a heart at peace gives life to the body, but envy rots the bones. And for some reason, you're fighting with Ruby, which isn't peaceful, and she's not the problem. You envy her relationship with your dad."

I squirmed, accidentally kicking Ruby's leg. She grunted and rolled to her side, going back to sleep, and I wondered about the guy who was supposed to meet her at the garden, hoping he'd left.

Earl folded his hands in his lap. "Envy steals your joy, Sally. Ruby never meant to cause you any harm. The problem with your unhappiness rests within you. It's your heart."

"I've gone through hard seasons. It's like Daddy's garden out there; when the weeds take over, the flowers die. I'm dead inside without Kyle and Kenny." I didn't finish and wept like dynamite blew up the reservoir of pain inside my soul.

Earl came to me, kneeling and holding my chin up. "Remember, Ruby has her walk, and you have yours. Max has enough love for both of you. Kyle and Kenny were gifts from God, too, so treasure those memories, but don't forget to live. Make Kyle proud and soar above this strife."

"I'm not good at making a difference. I'm good at shredding things up and destroying stuff."

"Now, being an only child didn't help you with sharing and showing kindness. But you've watched your dad show this to others. His goodness to Ruby shouldn't surprise you."

"Daddy is good to everyone. He sees a need, and he responds to it."

Earl encouraged me, "He's going to come home in a few days, and he may struggle with his health. But there are plenty of good days left for you and your dad. Cherish this time."

"Yes, sir." I thought about how soon Daddy would take the sunflower seeds from the dead blooms and store them over the winter to plant in the spring. I looked at Earl. "It's time for me to come out of my winter and plant myself and grow."

"Yes, it's time for you to return to the Sally I once knew. Those cats fighting for their territory outside remind me of you and Ruby. It's time for you to let go of the fight and rest in knowing you have your dad's love, and it lasts forever. That will not change."

"But I get so mad at Ruby. She's a thorn in my side."

He laughed. "Maybe you're a thorn in her side, too."

"Yeah, I'm sure that's true." I rubbed my burning eyes; my mouth dried from too much talking. "I'm getting a drink and going to bed. You are going home tonight, right, Earl?"

He yawned, stretching his arms. "No, I'll sleep in this chair and make sure you two get through the night. The sun will bring new challenges, enough for the day. Let's get some rest."

I slid my feet across the floor, knocking off my tennis shoes and leaving them by the dining room table. I touched a jar of jam, whispering to the label, "Daddy, you better get better and fast. We have Pioneer Days coming up."

Turning on the water at the kitchen faucet, I gulped down two glasses of water and marched to the screened-in porch, sitting on the cot, gazing at the shadows of darkness, and I didn't see the man waiting for Ruby.

Crossing my legs, I decided to take a moment to pray, to make time for focusing on what God might have me do. My prayer swirled from deep down, and the verse Ruby shared earlier did touch my heart, but I didn't want her to know it for some reason. "Dear God, move the things that are in my way. Show me how to return to my upbringing and let me make my daddy proud."

As I rose, about to topple over with a need for sleep, I tiptoed into the living room, and Earl's feet came into view, revealing he'd met the sandman and lounged in the recliner.

I glanced at the couch where the blanket lay tumbled into a mess, Ruby's spot empty. I yawned, unable to yell, my strength drained. "Well, that figures. Ruby's gone. Now Daddy's going to blame me for this, too."

I pushed the cracked front door wider, peering into the dark.

Earl mumbled, half asleep. "She's gone, isn't she? Well, isn't that what you wanted?"

"Wanted?"

"To have your dad all to yourself?"

"Yes, but no. Not this way."

I Promise

After a couple of nights of fitful sleep and tossing and turning, the roller coaster ride of emotions zapped me, but I kept searching for Ruby. I've checked all over town, and not one person knows one thing about where Ruby hides out. This is a small town. So how can Ruby be here and not be seen?

On Tuesday morning, I wanted to find Rick and Jeanne from the Bible study, but they headed out for a vacation early. I never got to ask them where she might go.

I carried Pearson's camera back to him at the newspaper later in the morning, too, and he promised to leave Ruby's wreck out of his paper for now. But he said it was conditional that I'd have to start freelancing for him, or he'd change his mind. I've agreed to start on Friday, with the first writing assignment to include a story about a hero in New Boston. The Chamber of Commerce plans to award a plaque of recognition to that person during the festival the following week, to be presented annually.

Still, I've wasted hours driving around to find Ruby so I could fix this before Daddy discovered the truth, that I'd run her off.

And now, it's sundown on Wednesday, and I'm parked at the Shell station again, hoping she shows herself.

Unfortunately, I have until tonight to find her, because Daddy's coming home tomorrow. Earl promised to give me time to reconcile this dilemma before he picked up Daddy, but I'm running low on options. And I'm desperate.

Tap. Tap. Tap.

The clerk hit my half-opened window with the ring on the back of his finger. "You can't come here and park every night. I told you Ruby comes here when she comes."

I rolled the window down the rest of the way. "And you don't have to hit my window every night. I purchased something as you said, and now I'm eating it in the parking lot. Is there a law against that?"

"No, there's no law. But how long does it take to eat a candy bar?"

"For me, longer than most people."

He threw his hands in the air. "If you want to find Ruby, try downtown in Texarkana, off Broad Street. She's friends with Katrina and Carl, who live at the homeless camps. She goes there when life gets too hard."

I yelled, "Why didn't you tell me that yesterday?"

"I'm under no obligation to tell you one thing. She'll return when she's ready."

"Great, now you're sending me off in the dark."

"Well, it's not like you haven't been here after dark each time I've seen you. If Ruby's there, she's there. Besides, the sun will rise again. I promise."

I tossed the Snickers wrapper into the floorboard and shut my window, putting my hand in front of the vent blowing the cool air into the vehicle. I was grateful to Earl, who fixed my air conditioning today, and I promised to pay him back when my check comes, which hopefully is soon.

He tossed the whiskey out for me and the cigarettes when he happened upon them inside the car at the body shop. Earl laughed when he told me the mechanic gave him an odd look when he carried whiskey and cigs to the trash can.

Turning toward the highway, I merged onto the ramp, heading to Texarkana. Daddy used to volunteer at a shelter near Broad and took me with him for years, so I'll drive near the camps and see if anyone's walking around and if they know Ruby.

Twenty minutes later, I idled my car beneath the bridge on Broad and stepped out, leaving my parking lights on. I called into the darkness. "Anyone out there? I'm looking for Katrina and Carl."

I leaned on the car after pacing up and down the road, and no one answered, not one person. I hollered again, "Is there anyone who knows Carl? How about Katrina?"

After thirty minutes or so, my nerves rattled me, and I imagined men lining up and coming for me, of knives shining in the shadows. I talked to myself. *What were you thinking? Anything could happen to you out here.*

I decided to give it one more shout. "Katrina. Carl. Ruby. Hello to anyone." I took a deep breath, ready to leave, when my foot tangled with some wire in the road. "Goodness, it's wrapped around my shoe."

As I unraveled the wire, it snapped back like a Slinky toy and zapped my leg, causing me to lose balance. I tripped, falling like a vase tossed from its shelf and landing face down, my chin scraping on the asphalt and my head bouncing like a ball. *Ugh!* "What in the world will happen next?"

I rolled to my side, blood gushing onto my hand when I touched my face, from my forehead and chin. I wept, my head pounding, and my body ached from the thud of toppling over. I shook on the ground, and the tears drenched my cheeks, mixing with the blood.

The physical pain sent me back in time to my car accident in Dallas, the one haunting me when I least expected it. That night it rained, and the storm dropped golf-ball-sized hail; the roads flooded within minutes.

Kyle and I had planned a picnic with Kenny at the park, only for the dark clouds to dump rain minutes after we unloaded the trunk with our blanket, picnic basket, and chairs. Before that evening ended, blood would run down my face too, and drench my heart with sorrow.

I insisted on driving us home since Kyle hated fighting the traffic on wet roads. I took the car over the overpass, the taller of the bridges crossing over Interstate 635, and the wind shifted, and the rain came at us from the side. At the top of the bridge, the car skidded sideways, and I lost control, sending the vehicle's passenger side crashing into the concrete barrier.

The sound of metal crunching and my son screaming, and Kyle's glare, is something I'll never forget. By the end of the night at the hospital, I was breathing, and my husband and son were gone.

I touched my head, coming back to the present, and sat with my back up against a tire. I screamed, "I'm sorry, Kyle. I'm so sorry, Kenny. I'm to blame. I did this to both of you. I should be punished or put away. I should have died that night."

A voice shattered the repetition of the horror story of my past. "Ma'am, are you all right?"

I winced, staring up at the face of a small woman with long hair, who was barefoot. "I might need a doctor." The blood dripped from my nose into my mouth and down my neck like a leaky pipe. I wiped my tongue on my shirt; the taste in my mouth was something like metal and ruined cheese mixed with hand sanitizer. I winced. "I tripped on this wire, and now I've cut my head and face."

"Your forehead has a pretty big gash. You need help. Do you have a phone?"

"Yes, inside the car. It's probably in the passenger seat."

"I'll call 911, but I'm going to the camp before the ambulance gets here. I don't like crowds."

I found myself reaching for her hand. "Is your name Katrina?"

She yanked free from my grasp. "How do you know my name?"

"I'm looking for Ruby. Someone told me you might know her and that you lived down here."

"You know Ruby Nell?"

I repeated with, "Yes, Ruby Nell."

"We're her family. Her full name is Ruby Nell Collins."

I begged for confirmation. "Is she brown-headed and about my size and age?" I wobbled to my feet, crouching to my knees. "Sorry, please call for help."

"Your phone wants a pass code."

"It's 1-2-4-5-7-8."

"Okay, I'm dialing 911 now." Katrina handed me the phone. "Here, tell them what's going on. I've got to go."

"But wait. Have you seen Ruby?"

"Yes, she's at our camp and staying with us. She had a run-in with someone in New Boston, a lady who accused her of things. A lady with red hair and a temper to match. Ruby had a bad wreck and is lucky to be alive."

I gulped, unsure how to tell Katrina I was the horrible lady from New Boston. But somehow, I think she knew.

Flashing lights showed on the top of the hill, and the ambulance moved closer, parking by my car. Katrina was already down the trail, and the two EMTs dashed to my side, putting pressure on my head with gauze and helping me onto a stretcher.

The rest of the night became a blur of bandages and stitches and X-rays and fluids in an IV. I tried to call Earl, but he never answered. My jeans were ripped, and my jaw ached with a pulse, a heartbeat of its own.

I signed some papers after a few hours and walked from the emergency room without a ride. Wadley Hospital is close to where I left my car, and I hoped the police hadn't towed it away. Too bad Daddy wasn't at this hospital because I could have slept in a chair in his room until morning.

I have a matching bandana of gauze around my head like Ruby's bandage since I also received thirty stitches close to my hairline near my right temple, and my chin is sporting a few stitches. The pounding inside my head feels like I have four hearts beating inside my skull.

In the parking lot, the security guard motored up next to me in his little golf cart. "Ma'am, do you need a lift to your car?"

"It's not here. The ambulance brought me, and I left my vehicle on Broad Street, close to Oak."

"That's a couple of blocks back over there, behind the library. That's a bit of a walk at this late hour."

"I don't have another way to get to my car. I'll have to walk."

The plump-faced man offered. "I get off in about fifteen minutes. Wait by the emergency room exit, and I'll give you a ride. I drive a white truck."

I didn't answer, my silence giving the guard my response.

He held the steering wheel. "I promise. You can ask inside at the emergency room desk. They'll vouch for me. I'm not dangerous. It's just a ride."

**

"Thank you. I appreciate your kindness."

The guard urged me. "Lock yourself in your car. And get home. You don't want to be out here by yourself. It's not safe."

I clicked the button on my key ring. "Thank you."

I waited for the guard to drive away in his truck, and I then tossed my keys into the driver's seat and stepped out, closing the door. I'm too close to finding Ruby; I must go and look for her.

I grabbed my cell and marched up the same trail Katrina disappeared on, and the overgrown grass shot up next to me like swords, ready to cut my arms off. I balanced on the uneven path, my head drumming along with each step.

I tapped the flashlight button on my cell phone, shining the light in front of me. I hollered, not loudly, quietly, but firm. "Katrina, it's me, the lady from earlier. I was hoping you'd let me talk to Ruby. Are you awake? Hello?"

I marched to the right, then the trail dipped lower to the left, and the water trickled in the stream beside me, keeping cadence with my heartbeat. "Hello, Katrina, it's me, Sally."

A flicker of a dot up ahead gave me hope. And a man's voice spouted off. "You should leave. Ruby's not up to seeing anyone."

"Carl, is that you?"

"Yes, it's me. Katrina told me about your accident, but you're not welcome down this path tonight. Or tomorrow."

I sighed, trying to say the right thing. "Tell Ruby, I've come to take her home. To my home, with me."

Carl shouted, "She's not going with you."

I panted, my breath shallow. "Please, tell Ruby our daddy is coming home from the hospital tomorrow."

"She doesn't have a dad. Try again."

"She has a new dad. He's my daddy. And he's her daddy. He has lung cancer, and he needs her at home." I slumped closer and closer and found myself about ten feet from a makeshift house facing a bearded man about the size of a small tree. "Carl, give me two minutes with her."

"She's asleep. We all should be asleep."

I bellowed, "Ruby, please come home with me. I'm sorry for everything. Please, I promise to do better. I promise to stop accusing you. I promise to keep my thoughts silent. I promise you won't have to run from my shouting or anger again. Please, come home."

Silence fell. Carl stopped talking, and he stood like a man sleepwalking. Katrina showed up next to him. And I waited.

The stream danced with its trickling music, and I prayed for Ruby to show herself to me on the path. But nothing, just Carl and Katrina watching me, watching them.

I turned and ran smack dab into Ruby. "So, you are up? And you're making me yell at you?"

"Yes." She pointed to my head. "What's that wrapped around your noggin?"

I smiled. "I'm just trying to be like you. Hey, maybe we can be twins."

"The only reason I'll come with you is so I can see Max. I'm not coming because of you."

"That's fine. Daddy will be thrilled to see you." I bit my tongue, wishing I meant what I said, and somehow, maybe I did. When I said thrilled, I didn't entirely choke on my words. And they did fall from my lips like jam from a spoon.

I followed Ruby down the trail toward the road, not realizing how far I'd come into the woods. The path wound around a thicket of bushes, and Ruby turned to me and whispered, "Max will be happy to see you, too. He always talked about how he wished you'd come home. He told me every story from your childhood and cried when he'd say your name, Sunflower."

I pulled on her sleeve. "You told me my daddy never talked about me in such a way."

"I might have said that to make you mad."

"Well, it worked. I was madder than you know what."

99

"Are you mad now?"

"No, I think this is the happiest I've been in a long time, knowing I found you and knowing he missed me." I hugged Ruby from behind. "Thank you for telling me how much he loves me."

"No one can take your spot. You're his pride and joy."

I grew ten inches in the dark on the inside because my heart took on a hopeful beat, and joy sneaked into my veins. "Thank you, Ruby. You made my year."

As we reached the road, stepping from the last bend, I dug inside my pants pocket. "Oh yeah, I left my keys in the seat."

Ruby yanked on my arm, motioning up and down the road as if giving instructions. "Sally, where is your car?"

New Beginnings

Daddy tucked his arms into the folds of his shirt across his belly, leaned back in his recliner, his feet high in the air, and wiggled his toes inside the orange socks with tacos on them. For the past hour, he'd grilled Ruby and me about our activities for the past couple of days, concerned we hadn't prevailed in maintaining weed control over our mouths and choices.

The Billy Graham rerun had Daddy's attention, too, his eyes flipping back and forth from the television as he absorbed the preacher's sermon, while taking in our validations and excuses for our behavior. Finally, Graham turned to one side of his mic, looking at the crowd. "God has given us two hands, one to receive with and the other to give with."

I smirked at Ruby and whispered, "Daddy's never watched this one."

Daddy glanced at me. "I've watched this a dozen times. Sometimes, repeating lessons is good for me."

I countered. "You mean, for me."

Ruby said, "I think he means all of us."

Daddy chuckled. "I might." He muted the remote. "Girls, tell me again how you both ended up at the homeless camps, and why you needed to call Pearson at 4 a.m. this morning?"

Ruby and I yawned in unison, our heads banged up, and our nightlife catching up with us. I licked the top of my lip, changing the subject. "Daddy, when did you start wearing colorful socks?"

He wiggled his toes, laughing, only to point his finger at me. "I see what you're doing. Changing the topic." He looked at his feet. "Earl bought these for me after I gave him the Pac Mac pajamas. You should see those PJs. He loves to parade around in them."

"He's proud of his jammies." Ruby snickered, her nose giving off a tired, wheezing sound. "Earl came over Monday night after ..." she paused, "after the wreck. He wanted to make sure we were safe."

I nodded, my eyes big, and raised my eyebrows. Maybe bigger eyes helped Ruby watch what she shared about our escapades. My confession followed as the truth rose. "Earl checked on us because we were arguing louder than Snowball and Charcoal, when the two of them tangled outside his window."

Daddy's eyebrows arched like mine. "Tell me what happened."

I unloaded like a girl with her hand caught, eating the last scoop of ice cream. "When I brought Ruby home from the hospital, we were met by her friend at the door. And he was a little aggressive."

Ruby butted in. "It was nothing. It was Seth." She turned to me. "I usually carry him a meal after Bible study. We hang out on Monday nights. When I didn't show, he was concerned. That's all. He talks hard, but he's a teddy bear."

I barked. "A teddy bear? He's a teddy bear with a Grizzly roar."

Ruby shifted, crossing her legs. "He's angry at the world like other people I know."

"I'm not as angry as I seem."

Daddy rubbed his chest. "Sally, you've been disgruntled for a long time."

I moved to his side. "Are you feeling okay?"

"Just some tightness. It comes and goes."

I whispered, "I'm not angry, but when someone lies to you, it can make you mad."

Ruby raised her hand, making a checkmark with her finger in the air. "See, Max. She's mad at me and you and the world."

I threw up my hands. "Ruby, you keep talking as if I'm not in the room."

Daddy clapped his hands. "Girls, we have a problem."

I nodded. "Do you need a doctor?"

"No, I'm tired. The problem is we need a vehicle, seeing as my truck is totaled, and yours is missing."

I smiled, trying to act chipper. "At least the air conditioning works for the person who stole my car. Unfortunately, I only had liability insurance, so I'll be walking for a while."

Daddy announced, "Well, Earl's taking me to the dealership after lunch. They have a black Silverado waiting for me on the back of the lot. It's like Pearson's truck."

"Do you feel well enough to go out?" I frowned, wishing Daddy's face didn't appear so pale.

Daddy inhaled, a long, purposeful breath. "Yes, time to get on with living."

"You'll love having a new truck."

"I've been saving my savings for way too long. I paid cash for the truck." He held his neck, coughing, clearing his throat. "Sally, I put money into your savings account this morning on the way home. You had $5 until I made a transfer."

"I haven't used my account at the credit union since high school."

"Now you have a little cash to get a car. And I opened a savings account for Ruby, too. She has five dollars less than you."

Ruby and I grinned at each other.

Daddy popped off with, "My daughters aren't walking."

Ruby wiped her eyes. "Max, I've never had a car."

"Well, there's enough in there for a small compact, but since I have reckless girls, I suggest both of you save a part of your money, in case you need a taxi." Daddy cocked his head, taking a sheet of paper from the end table where he keeps his airplane stash. He creased the sides, tweaking the wings. And then sailed the paper airplane across the room. "Be careful where you fly and where you land."

I picked up the paper airplane. "Very funny. We won't need a taxi."

Ruby piped in. "We might. Sally's pretty careless."

I switched topics, something I'm good at in my family. "So Ruby, what's the real story with Seth?"

She patted her head; her right eye twitched. "You are so nosy. At our Bible study, we have leftover snacks and sandwiches. I take Seth some and encourage him to join the men's study on Wednesday nights. But he's not interested, well, not yet."

"Tell the truth."

"I'm telling you the truth."

"But Seth got in your face and said you, and he needed to talk. He didn't come to the house because he was hungry."

Ruby shrugged her shoulders. "You've misunderstood him. Seth's overcoming his past and saying what he means gets lost in his words. He's in a tight place and trying to pay off his debts."

I finished the part she left out. "And he comes to you for money."

"Sometimes, I help when I can. I owe him."

"Owe him? I knew it; he's pressuring you."

Daddy pushed down the recliner's handle, sitting straight up. "Seth moved in with his grandma last year, right after he got out of jail."

I wiggled in my seat. "Why was he in jail?"

Daddy cleared his throat. "For stealing a car."

I coughed. "Now, there's some irony. Maybe he snatched mine."

Ruby defended him. "He's changing. Like I am. He just needs a chance."

"I was teasing. I didn't say Seth took my car."

"You did too. Do you even listen to what you say?" Ruby rubbed her head. "Seth and I go back ten years."

I interrupted her, "I knew he wasn't your brother."

"No, he's not. And I told you that. We're about the same age, though."

I sighed. "So how old are you?"

"I'm going to be forty-one in October, not that it matters."

"I was curious, that's all."

"You're nosey."

I bounced my shoulders like a toddler. "I can be. So, tell me, why would you owe him, as you put it?"

"Seth is the reason I'm alive."

"What? This is too weird."

Ruby wiped a tear from her eye. "He saved me from ending my life one night. I had planned to jump from the bridge into the Red River, and as God, that's what Max says," she glanced at Daddy, smiling. "As God would have it, Seth sped down the highway driving a stolen truck. He'd taken it from a ball field and headed north down Highway 8 at the same time I wanted to die."

"What? So, he's a savior and a thief, all in one?"

"Something like that."

Daddy added, "God uses strange situations to help us trust Him."

I nudged Ruby with my foot from my end of the couch. "What happened next?"

"Seth raced by me in the car but spun out as he crossed the bridge. While trying to get the wheels out of the ditch, Seth found himself charging toward me on foot. He spoke to me about living and challenged me to step away from the edge. He risked getting caught by the police, which I didn't know at the time."

"That river has currents that will suck you under. I can't believe it. So Seth saved your life?"

"Yes, he did. Really."

"Unreal. I'm sorry you wanted to end your life; what an amazing rescue."

"I know, I was shocked. The patrol cars arrived with their lights flashing, and Seth was handcuffed while I hid behind the trees. He didn't think they'd believe me if I said I hadn't been in the car with him since we were so far out of town."

Daddy added his part. "A good man is living inside Seth. I believe God will use him for great things soon."

I turned to Ruby. "Wow, I'm impressed by how God used a crime to give you life. And then He used a snake to put us together. And again, you're still alive."

Ruby shrugged. "I've always wanted someone to care about me. Seth showed me a glimpse of what kindness felt like, and later, I met Max."

I turned to Daddy. "By the way, where did you meet Ruby?"

"I sort of ran into her with my truck after she stole some strawberries from my garden."

Ruby argued, "I didn't steal your berries. I offered to work off the meal."

Daddy smiled. "But that was after your tummy was packed full of luscious strawberries."

"I sort of ate before asking for permission."

"True, but we worked it out."

I brought Daddy back to my question. "What? How did you run over Ruby?"

"Well, she stepped in front of my truck when I pulled from the gas pumps one night. She was under the front fender, without a scratch. I bought her orange juice, and we became friends, even if it took me buying gas there each week to talk to her."

I chuckled with an evil tone. "No way, you bought Ruby a snack?"

"Yes, she was thirsty and needed a healthy drink, not soda."

I shook my head at Ruby. "And yet, you argued with me when I offered you snacks the other night. What's that about?"

"Max has kind eyes. I didn't like how you looked at me."

I shivered. "My eyes can be piercing. But you weren't terribly friendly yourself."

"I'd had a bad day. It happens."

Daddy used our discussion to drive home a point. "Both of you are fearfully and wonderfully created in the image of God. Unique. And special. Somewhat troubled. But filled with promise."

I soaked up my daddy's wise words. "It's great to be home. I love you, Daddy."

"I love you, too, Sunflower. The house is better with you here." Daddy glanced at Ruby. "Did Seth pay his grandma's rent? I gave you his pay for working on the crates for the jam."

"Yes, I gave him the $50."

I meddled. "When did you do that?"

"When you were behind me in the yard the other night."

Daddy smiled. "Good, I know he needs it." He took the conversation back. "Girls, you haven't told me what sent you to Texarkana and why you, Sally, left your keys in your car."

I mouthed, "I'd run Ruby off and worried you'd never forgive me. So, I looked for her for two days. Finally, the store clerk told me to check the camps. I had planned to drive right back, but after I stomped up the trail calling for Ruby, I kept going when I saw the light. I found her at Carl and Katrina's camp. I never thought anyone would steal my car."

Daddy pulled Ruby into our talk and came over and sat with us on the couch. "Why did you leave? You know you're welcome here."

"It's complicated. Since Sally came home, life has gotten difficult."

"But running away never solves anything." Daddy touched his forehead, then pointed to mine. "Sally, how did you get those stitches on your head?"

"I tripped, like I've done a hundred times. My feet got tangled, and the wire zapped me, and I crashed to the pavement like a cinder block."

"You both could stand to stay home and do less roaming."

Ruby agreed. "I've been better here than anywhere. But I've gotten distracted this week."

I interjected, "I'm somewhat distracted too. I've been running from life since Kenny and Kyle died. I may have stitches on my head, but my heart has been bleeding for months and months. The guilt from the wreck has weighed on me. I've lived as a prisoner to that night."

Ruby sat up, staring at me with tears in her eyes. "I'm sorry. We all have hard days. Huh?"

I nodded, breathing through my mouth. "It takes my breath away when I think of my husband and son suffering."

Daddy added, "Loss is hard. Love is, too. It takes time to heal, but hurting others is never right."

"Yes, I know." I pouted a little, knowing I've struggled with my mouth for too long.

Ruby smiled, putting her feet on the floor and scooting closer to Daddy, but looking at me. "Max has told me the same thing."

I grinned. "He twists words to make a point."

"I twist my words to help you live."

Ruby hugged Daddy, and then I grabbed his neck too. "Daddy, I start work tomorrow for Pearson. I'll pay my way."

Daddy stood. "The money's a gift, and the way you can pay me back is for you and Ruby to offer each other friendship, the kind that holds each person accountable while showing love. That's the only payment I need."

Ruby teased. "I have to love her?"

I argued, "But I just met Ruby. We need time."

Daddy shook his head. "Start with friendship. As for time, it's no better than today. Begin there."

Ruby hugged Daddy harder, and since I'm not to be outdone, I reached around his neck with my spaghetti arms, kissing him on the cheek.

He grabbed his chest. *Whoa!*

I held onto Daddy. "Are you sure you're okay?"

Ruby got in his face. "Take a deep breath. Come on."

Pam Kumpe

A Broken Sunflower

While Daddy rested in his bed, Ruby and I checked on him by circling through his room. She popped in through the porch door, and I popped in through the bathroom. First, I bent down to see if he was breathing, then Ruby pressed her fingers on his wrist to feel for a pulse. Finally, we nodded and left the room.

A few minutes later, I shuffled up to the bed, watching his chest rise and fall. He finally shooed me from the bedroom, assuring me he was only tired.

Ruby and I wiggled in our seats in the living room, and I watched the muted TV from Daddy's recliner. "This must be a Billy Graham marathon. He's preaching all day."

"Your dad introduced me to Billy Graham. I'd never heard of him." Ruby marched over to me, yanking the remote from the end table. "By the way, it's a DVD. This is your dad's favorite sermon series."

"Well, there you go. A DVD series."

I curled up in the chair in desperate need of sleep, and Ruby crashed on the couch, using my daddy's favorite throw. About the time I settled in and dozed for a while, I heard Daddy rummaging in the kitchen, whistling and humming, alternating his tunes, originals I didn't recognize.

I opened one eye, listening to him talk to himself. "I'm ready for a grilled cheese sandwich with syrup. Let's see. Hey, do you girls want one?" He called to us as if we were awake and ready for food.

I popped up, sliding into the kitchen next to Daddy. "I'll make them. You sit and rest."

"It's three in the afternoon, and we've missed lunch. Earl's taking me at four to get my truck."

"Well then, put your taco-socks up and watch TV. Or make a paper airplane."

Ruby joined me, wiping her eyes and yawning. "I'm good at pouring syrup."

I grunted. "It takes no talent to pour syrup from a dispenser."

She countered, laughing like a squeaky toy. "It takes no talent to slap cheese between two pieces of bread, either."

I nudged her like a sister might if I'd had one. I wrapped my fingers around the iron skillet Daddy placed on the stovetop. He didn't let go.

He argued, "I've got this under control."

I yanked the skillet to the other burner. "We'll take care of lunch. Now enjoy this, but don't get used to it."

"Sunflower, when was the last time you cooked a meal of any kind?"

Ruby answered for me. "She probably buys fast food."

"You have no idea what I do or don't do."

"I know you eat junk food from gas stations."

"I do not."

"You do too, and you even bought me junk food."

We tangled our words while Daddy melted butter in the hot skillet; our continuous hot words flew from our mouths as if we needed splatter guards on our faces.

Daddy shushed us. "Girls, I can do this before you two figure out where the butter is in the fridge and before you get the plates from the cupboard."

Ruby kicked the cabinet door, the loose one that bounced back and hit her leg. "Stupid door."

Daddy added, "Kicking things never solved anything."

"I was kicking it so I wouldn't say another ugly word to Sally."

I mouthed, "Well, this kitchen's not big enough for all three of us."

"Both of you find something productive to do. I'm making four grilled cheese sandwiches, two for me and one for each of you. In the meantime, the cats are meowing at the back door. Has anyone fed them? And the garden needs watering. We didn't get much rain Sunday night, and I want the sunflowers to keep blooming for the rest of what summer we have left."

"I'll feed the cats," Ruby said, reaching under the sink for a bag of cat food.

"I'll water the garden."

Daddy hummed another tune I didn't know while Ruby and I slipped outside. Ruby petted Charcoal and Snowball, and they meowed for the cat food. "Yes, Ruby loves you."

I mouthed. "You do love these cats, I see."

"They love me too." She shook the bag of cat food. "Because I have what they want."

"I may get a kitten someday. I haven't had a cat in forever."

"You don't need a cat. You'd forget to feed it."

I shook my head, watching Ruby pour cat food into the bowl. And Snowball and Charcoal shared a meal as if they'd forgotten the fight from this week.

Ruby petted their heads. "Good food. And nice kitties."

I unwound the garden hose by the side of the house, pulling it across the yard to the garden. "Hey, Ruby, will you turn the water on?"

"Are you serious? Can't you turn the water on yourself?" She petted Charcoal, only for Snowball to nudge her with his nose.

"So much for this new friendship." I snapped.

Daddy stuck his head out the screen door in time to hear us. "How many lessons on kindness will you two need?"

Before we could engage and continue arguing, Earl's voice sailed from his backyard. "Hello, neighbors."

I couldn't see him since he was behind the sunflowers.

Earl said, "I could hear Sally and Ruby exchanging harsh words from inside my house."

I yelled, "I'm sure your windows are open."

"They are wide open. I don't like paying to run my air conditioning when I can cool off with a breeze."

"Earl, it's August and almost 100 degrees. You have the money to pay your electric bill. Turn on the air."

"This may be true. But I choose what to waste and what to save." Earl showed up at the end of the garden near the tomato plants. "You two are so headstrong. And you speak before thinking."

I rushed to the water spigot and turned it on. "She's worse."

Ruby hollered from the steps. "I am not."

Earl laughed. "I've made my point."

I countered. "I simply asked Ruby to turn on the water, and she barked at me."

"I didn't bark. I chose not to turn the water on."

Earl folded his hands like he might pray, his long legs taking double strides. "Ruby, imagine if you had chosen the other option."

She rolled her eyes, and I rolled mine.

Daddy waved at us. "The grilled cheese sandwiches are waiting for us. Come on. Let's eat." He motioned to Earl. "Come in; we'll run to the dealer and get my truck after I eat a bite."

To get the last word or the last spray, I pulled on the hose, my hands twitching like I was ten again. I placed a finger over the end of the mist, shooting water at Ruby, missing her by inches.

She yelled, "Stop that; you'll regret getting me wet."

I shot a spray of water into the air, the sun dissecting the drops, revealing a rainbow above me, and the droplets cooled me off. I challenged Ruby. "And what will you do if I get closer and you get soaked?"

Ruby put her hand up. "Stop. Don't move another foot." Ruby hopped from the steps, backing away.

"So, you're afraid of a little water?"

"No, but you'd better turn around and see what's behind you."

"Right, there's nothing behind me; you want to rush me and take the hose."

"Why would I come toward you? I don't want to get wet."

Earl swung his giraffe legs wide and moved to the steps near Daddy, whose laugh jiggled his stomach, and his eyes lit up the county. His chuckles triggered mine, and then Earl's and finally Ruby's giggles squealed along with ours.

Our crowing hushed the blue jays in the nearby tree, and my hand swiped up like a cheerleader doing a cheer, and the water drenched Earl.

He touched his shirt, pausing for a second, only to pick up steam. "Sally, I didn't come over here to take a bath."

"Sorry, not sorry." I ran to turn the hose off before getting everyone wet.

Daddy reached for his chest again, like earlier, gulping in a deep breath. His wheezing became louder than the chatter and laughter. We all stopped moving, except for the trickle of water splashing my tennis shoes. "I'm sorry. Daddy, are you sure you're all right?"

"My breath is short, and my chest feels as if a bowling ball landed on my rib cage. Let's eat. I need to sit for a minute."

I grabbed the cast-iron skillet in the kitchen, putting it in the soapy water, while Daddy carried his plate and glass of tea to his chair. Earl joined him in the living room, turning Billy Graham on, the volume at a decibel that made me rub my ears.

Ruby scooted to the cot on the back porch, eating alone, sitting by herself, saying she needed some space.

I squished in my wet shoes, leaving small dabs of water on the linoleum floor. Finally, I smacked my grilled cheese at the counter, dabbing each bite of crust in syrup and swishing the goo around in my mouth.

Cough. Cough. Cough.

I leaned into the doorway, looking toward the living room, staring over the jam on the dining room table. "Daddy, are you all right?"

"I'm good. The syrup gagged me."

I licked my fingers. "Okay. Thank you for the grilled cheese. I haven't had one in years."

"You're welcome. I've got a little more syrup on my plate. Can't waste a drop."

Earl chimed in. "That's right, never waste food."

Ruby returned to the kitchen, opening the fridge. "I need some tea." She hollered, "Max, do you need a refill? Earl?"

Daddy called, "No, I've still got some."

Earl showed up next to us with ice clinking in the glass. "Sure, I'm hot. Can't get cool today."

I wrinkled my nose. "It's because you don't run the air conditioning in your house."

Earl grumbled, "It's hot in the summer. Period."

Ruby pulled out the pitcher. "Here you go, Earl. Cool off and ignore little Miss Sally and her sharp tongue."

He leaned on the wall by the stove, sipping his drink. "August days make me thirsty." Earl touched my shoulder and

Ruby's. "Ladies, hold onto these simple days. They make the best memories. Max is one of a kind. He's given much to this community. His example can be one to follow."

I agreed, my heart full, my shoes wet, and my tears returning. "I sure love my daddy. He's good to me when I'm bad, and when I'm good, he's better to me than I deserve. He doesn't let me get away with things, but he's gentle when he corrects me."

Ruby moved next to me, and her countenance shone with a look of joy. "You've been fortunate to have him. He's a part of you. And at times, I see him in you." She paused, almost like she didn't mean to say the last part. "I'm thankful to be a small part of his life."

"I've taken so much for granted. My daddy's a gift from God."

Ruby nodded. "Not all dads are great fathers."

Earl patted Ruby on the shoulder. "Max has given you his love, something Sally's had all along." He turned to me. "I remember how Max made a great mom too, not just a dad, except when he braided your hair when you were a small girl. We got my Minnie to fix your hair after that disaster."

I smiled, "Yes, he did more than any girl could ask."

Earl placed his empty glass on the counter after gulping the second refill down. "Well, we'd better get that truck. Your dad's driven by the lot every day lately, looking at his prize, hoping to buy a new truck. And now Ruby's wreck moved him into deciding, one he wanted to make anyway. We'll be back before you know it."

As Earl moved to the living room, Ruby peered through the side of the porch toward the sunflowers. "Hey, when you were watering us, I think you accidentally snapped the top of a sunflower. The flower is broken and hanging down."

I wiped my hands on a paper towel. "No way. I couldn't have done it. The water pressure was low, and I never got that close to the flowers. I never really got to watering the garden before we came inside to eat."

Earl stopped in the dining room, looking back. "Maybe the heat's been too much."

"Or maybe you snapped the top of the sunflower." Ruby danced to the porch. "I bet you did it. You're quite the reckless one."

I chuckled, "Reckless one? You're the one who wrecked a truck."

"And if you'll remember, it was because of a snake. A snake will cause you to do things like crash into a sign." Ruby waved her arms as if she were tired of explaining herself to me.

Earl shouted from the living room, catching my attention. "Sally, your daddy needs a doctor!"

The Secret's Out

I charged to the front of the house. "No!"

Earl held Daddy's wrist. "Sally, where's your cell?" He tore by me to the phone in the dining room. "Move out of the way. He's unconscious but breathing, and he needs help now."

I froze next to the recliner, my hands gripped together, my heart pounding in my neck. "Daddy?" Ruby shadowed me, not saying a word, but she took his hand in hers, weeping with sobs louder than the preaching on the TV.

Daddy's head lay twisted to one side, and he clasped a paper airplane. His glass of tea toppled over, and the ice cubes on the floor. And one of his socks hung from his toes, almost off.

Rushing to my bedroom, I fumbled for my phone in case Earl wasn't successful on the house phone, but I didn't dial when I heard him asking for an ambulance. "Yes, please hurry."

Pacing, I lost reality, my head spinning, and I jumped outside to the porch. "Where's that ambulance?"

Earl said, "They're on the way. And don't block the doorway."

"I won't." Back beside Daddy's recliner, I wept, the shaking of my knees like tremors from an earthquake. "No, Daddy, stay with us. Please don't leave; we're finally together. Things are good. I just got home. Don't forget, your truck is waiting for you."

I fell to my knees, and Ruby stood close, hovering like a statue. She cried, "Max, you're the daddy I never had. Stay, don't leave now."

For what seemed like the longest inhale of my life, I exhaled my childhood where I pedaled my bicycle up and down our street. I exhaled a memory of holding the fishing pole at the lake and fighting off squirmy worms when they fell from my fingers. I remembered my one attempt at playing softball, only to quit the team in week two and opt for writing stories instead.

I jumped to my teen years, with my induction into the National Honor Society and the two weeks I spent on the tennis team, which I quit since I wasn't athletic.

My mind hurried to college, to studying, to writing stories, to meeting Kyle, to our wedding, and then to giving birth to my son, Kenny. My next exhale took me to the car wreck, bringing me to the present day, to this horrible, terrible moment with Daddy in his chair—unconscious.

I'd captured the longest and shortest of my memories like a rerun on a DVD. And many included the best dad a girl could hope for.

A few flashbacks jumped into my thoughts of my leaving small-town life, and how, in some ways, I'd excluded my daddy when he was everything to me.

He loved me from the moment I took my first breath, or so he always told me. He kissed my forehead a million times at night when I went to bed. And he didn't know it, but when I pushed curfew in high school, I often saw him drive by checking on me. I'd leave and head for home, driving up almost before he had time to get into the house.

I longed for one more day, for one more hour. For one more chance to watch him plant his vegetables and flowers in the spring. To see him smile when the tomatoes were red. When the strawberries were plush. To sit with him and eat fried okra. To eat our ice cream at night again. To help him sell jam at Pioneer Days. To feel his arms around me, telling me, "You're Daddy's girl. I'd pick you from the garden first."

I felt my chest tighten. Could cancer snap my daddy from me before I could inhale again, like a sunflower that lost its blooms?

The following minutes turned into a blur as the EMTs hurried into our house, testing and prodding and putting an oxygen mask on Daddy's face. Finally, they loaded him into the stretcher, with more poking and prodding, checking for life.

I ran up to the back of the ambulance. "Is he going to make it?"

The door slammed, and the ambulance drove off as Ruby stepped into the road like a robot, and then she made her way next to me, taking my hand in hers. I squeezed hers back, and Earl waved at us from his car, motioning us to come on.

Ruby hopped into the front seat, and I fell into the back. I shouted, "Earl, will he live?"

"I'm not sure. Just pray. Pray for your daddy."

We flew downtown, ran the red light, rushed to Highway 8, and then toward the ramp to the interstate, passing semi-trucks and rushing up behind vehicles in the fast lane. Earl hollered, "Hey, get out of our way! No, don't slow down. Hey, buddy, use your blinker next time."

Ruby consoled Earl. "Calm down and stop yelling at the drivers in the other cars."

"I'm sorry, I'm stressed. We need to get to the hospital. And we need to pray."

I touched his shoulder from my seat. "Earl, be careful. We don't need to wreck your car." A twitch of pain on my forehead from my stitches made me wince, and I found myself glancing at Ruby, whose entire head was mainly a bandage of gauze.

I swallowed hard, the sorrow caught in my throat, gagging me. I prayed, holding my neck. "Dear God, please let my daddy live. Let the doctors save him."

At the hospital, Earl parked the car, and we raced inside to the emergency room. We weren't allowed back to Daddy's room, and we fidgeted in the chairs, and then we paced, and I kept asking if we could go back; each time the answer was no.

Earl went to the counter as a shift change brought a new person to the desk. "I'm Pastor Earl Milton. Will you tell me what room Max Williams is in?"

His calmness and smooth words got a smile from the lady, and she touched the screen on her computer, tapping the monitor. "He's in number 3; go down that hallway." She pointed as if she allowed royalty to go behind the double doors.

I bolted up next to Earl just before the doors shut. "Can I go with you?"

He turned to me, using a low voice. "I'm going back as pastoral care, so let me see what I can learn."

I went numb, my arms like rubber, and I didn't want to lose control, but my daddy's too far from me. My feet were having trouble staying in the waiting room. I was close to pretending I was a preacher, too. I turned to my almost-sister. "Ruby, what are we going to do?"

"I'm not sure. We knew this day was coming. Max has been sick for a year." She put her hand to her mouth as if she dropped a bomb on my heart, an explosion imminent.

I plopped down in the chair next to her, my hands waving in the air. "For a year? No, that's not right. My letter from Earl said Daddy found out about his lung cancer a few weeks ago, and he encouraged me to come home."

"I'm sorry. It slipped out. I didn't mean to say anything."

"What? Seriously, he's been sick for a while?"

"Yes, your dad's diagnosis came last summer, after Pioneer Days."

"That's not true. He would have told me."

"Max didn't believe the doctor at first. But right after Pioneer Days, Earl noticed your dad couldn't get his breath when we packed up the crates in his truck. Earl insisted your dad get a checkup." Ruby wiped the snot from her nose with the back of her hand.

I cried, "This is insane. Why didn't anyone tell me?"

"I'm not supposed to tell you. It wasn't my story to tell."

I nudged her so hard she slid to the floor from her chair.

"What are you thinking?" Ruby got on her knees and pulled herself up. "Stop putting your hands on me when you're mad."

I begged, "It's a reflex. Sorry. But why couldn't you tell me?"

"Actually, I didn't know you didn't know, well, not for sure, until Earl told me he mailed you the letter last week. As for telling you, we didn't quite start on the right foot, remember?"

"True, but he's been sick for a year?"

Ruby stood in front of me, her bandage sliding from her head sideways. She pulled it off, revealing a bruise across her forehead the size of a grapefruit. She held the gauze, winding it up into a ball. "Your dad's original diagnosis came close to the week that marked the first anniversary of you losing Kyle and Kenny."

I wrung my hands together, not pleased with the puzzle piece they'd kept from me. I hated that August held too many sad stories for one family to bear. I spat, "Daddy talked to you about his cancer and not me, and you kept this a secret for a whole year?"

"I'm not the one who should have told you."

"But, look, now you have. And even Earl kept the secret until he wrote the letter with only a partial truth."

"He didn't lie. Earl said you must know before it's too late, and he didn't want you to hear about your dad's cancer after he passed away."

I shoved Ruby, and she stumbled backward, and I mouthed, "Seriously, this is crazy." I pointed my finger at her. "He's my daddy, don't you ever forget it. He's not yours. You've had all this time with him while I was three hours away."

"It's not like you come home anyway. You were gone for an entire two years. Remember?"

A security guard marched up. "Ladies, you'll need to bring it down a notch. Why don't you take your conversation outside? You're causing a commotion."

I folded my arms, stomping to the parking lot, hissing like a cat, ready to plant my claws into Ruby. She followed me, explaining, "You're overreacting. Your dad didn't want to worry you. He was protecting you."

I swatted at the mosquitoes and hoped I hit Ruby instead. "But you knew. And Earl knew. And yet, you kept me in the dark."

"Wait, I didn't even know you a week ago. This isn't on me. Your dad cared about your emotional well-being."

"To leave me out is wrong, and mean, and outright horrible."

"It's not mean. Your dad was worried about how you might handle the news."

"It makes no sense. I'm his daughter." I stormed between the parked cars, hollering and crying and making more noise than a lion roaring at its prey.

After minutes and minutes of my shouting, Ruby ran up to me, keeping a car between us, probably for her safety. "Earl's come for you. He's over there."

"What does he want? I'm in no mood to talk to either of you."

"Your dad's awake. He's asking for you."

I darted between the cars and toward Earl. "Daddy's awake? Can I see him?"

"Yes, he's in and out, but he's asking for you." I gave Earl an evil glare. "Well, take me to him. Please."

We stepped into the small room where Daddy turned his head my way on the makeshift bed, which wasn't much bigger than a stretcher. He lifted his hand, only for his arm to go right down. "Come here, Sunflower."

I almost snapped, but his eyes cut deep into my soul, revealing a love-glance that no other person has ever given me. "Daddy, why? Why didn't you let me come home before now and help take care of you? And be with you?"

He whispered, "You were getting on your feet at your job at the paper. And you were already hurting so much. I couldn't add another burden to your life."

"You're never a burden. I'm your daughter." A sour knot balled up in my stomach, and the tears slid from my eyes. "Daddy, I love you."

Daddy whispered, his words low. "I love you more than a garden of sunflowers, and you are the best thing I've done on this earth. But Sunflower, if you wish to be happy for a moment ..."

I sniffled, finishing his sentence. "... take a nap."

He gave a slight grin. "If you wish to be happy for a day ..."

"I know this one too … go fishing or plant a garden of sunflowers."

Daddy held my hand. "If you wish to be happy for a lifetime …"

I rubbed my nose. "I've forgotten that one."

Earl finished Daddy's last sentence. "... help someone and share the goodness of God."

I gave Earl an ugly glance and turned back to my daddy. "You should have told me you were sick."

"I regret keeping this from you. But you've had your struggles."

"I know, but I would have come. I would have."

Daddy faded out, closing his eyes, and Earl put his arm around my shoulder. "I'm sorry. I've broken your confidence in me."

"Is he asleep?"

"Yes, he'll rest. They're keeping him."

"I pray he comes home again. I'm not ready to say goodbye."

"We all love Max."

Sighing, I looked back over my last two years, knowing full well I've wavered between panic attacks and screaming at everyone, to sleeping for days at a time, to not sleeping for nights. I've not lived with joy for a long time. And I've wasted days and months and time with my daddy.

Earl took my hand. "Let's go home. They'll call if we should come, but for tonight, he'll need the rest."

I wrapped my hand around Earl's long fingers. "A part of me understands why no one told me. But I'm not happy about it."

The rest of the visit evolved into another cloud of activity. The doctor came in. "We'll admit him to intensive care and get him stable. And we'll keep you posted on his progress."

I realized Ruby hadn't come inside with us. "Where did Ruby go?"

"She offered to stay outside, to give you this time."

I cackled. "That was nice of her."

"She's not your enemy."

"I know. I'm trying to come to terms with how close she is to Daddy."

**

In the car on the way home, no one talked, and no one cried. I became a zombie stuck in the season of a 'possible goodbye,' and nothing seemed real. The noise of my questions rattled in my head, and landslides of worry crashed into my skull.

Earl parked in my driveway and let us out, and in the shadows of sunset, I methodically marched to the water hose, giving the sunflowers a good watering since I'd not finished the task earlier. My tears puddled on the ground, a shower of sadness, mixing with the muddy water. "I don't want to say goodbye to Daddy. This can't be happening."

I peeked across the yard at Ruby as she sat on the steps by the back porch. She hadn't spoken since the parking lot scene, but now she's humming a tune while sitting off to my side. A song she knew, but I didn't.

And then, like a match lit a fire beneath her, burning her rear end, Ruby shouted, "I'm gone. I can't be here right now."

I called her. "You can't go now. Please, stay. I need someone to stay with me tonight. Please."

Ruby ignored me and kept walking, and I tossed the hose down. "Wait, please, you must be here when we go pick up Daddy."

"I can't watch him die. I can't lose him. If I leave, I can imagine him alive and here at this house." Ruby took off down the road until she disappeared out of sight.

I kept calling, "No, stay. Please stay. Don't leave again."

Don't Touch Me

Earl called to me from his front porch. "Let her go. We all deal with grief differently. She thinks she's in the way. She'll be all right."

"How do you know she'll be fine? I was left to myself when Kyle and Kenny died; I could have used some counseling."

"I checked on you for your dad many times. I mailed you cards and scriptures for most of a year or more. You never responded; it's as if you were caught in the reeds of a lake, and your sorrow swallowed you up. Your tone was harsh on the phone, and you were short with your dad. It crushed him to see you like that, and it hurt him more whenever he did talk to you. We didn't know what to do, except we constantly prayed for you."

I marched across the driveway to his yard. "I could have used my daddy by my side. He could have come to Dallas."

"Never forget how he offered, and you hung up on him every time he wanted to come, and you even screamed for him to leave you alone."

"I was in a bad place." I swallowed hard, unable to justify myself or my behavior. Taking a good look at myself was a horror of embarrassment, and I was ashamed of how selfish I'd become.

"Your dad knew you were hurting, but don't ever forget he lost your mother when you were six months old."

"Yes, he's known loss too." I cried, "But I need him."

"Take life a breath at a time. Follow your dad's lead. Take a hard look in the mirror and ask God to soften your heart, to give you joy again."

I processed the conversation and Earl's explanations. He was right. Whenever I look in the mirror, I don't see a person who is fun to be around. I've spent days and weeks hurting others with my words.

I swallowed and glanced up the street toward the pavilion. I worried about Ruby, a rare emotion for me. "But, Earl, Ruby might not have a place to stay."

"She'll go to Seth's grandmother's house. I'll call over there after a bit to check on her."

I shook my head. "I still don't know how she found a way to the camps in Texarkana the other night. It's not like she has a bike or even a car."

"Well, you don't have a car either."

"No kidding."

"As for Ruby, she's friends with several from church who do street ministry with the homeless. She may have gotten a ride with one of them."

"Did she use to live with Carl and Katrina?"

"She lived near them in the past. Once Ruby had an apartment, but she suffers from paranoia. While riding the city bus to work in Texarkana, she thought the new driver was her late father. He used to yell and beat her, along with her mother. She got off the bus and never rode it again, and lost her job at the hotel where she worked in the laundry. That put her back in the camps."

"How sad. How terrible to be that afraid."

Earl used my comment to validate her need for my daddy. "Max is an example of the goodness of God, and he gives Ruby hope. When she's here, she's not so afraid."

"I've judged her. But I think she's guilty of judging me too."

129

"Yes, you both are quite complicated and needy, and neither of you is great at sharing Max."

"I'm needy?" I touched my chest. "Not me."

Earl smiled, leaning on the rail of the porch. "Come around to the other side of my house. I've got something to show you."

"What, right now? I'm tired. I'm going to take a bath and eat ice cream."

"Well, it can wait."

I strutted across the yard, the crunchy brown grass breaking beneath my shoes. "This grass isn't going to make it."

"Yeah, the weather's hotter this summer. The other night felt like a spring rain in August. Big drops. But not many."

As I walked around Earl's concrete driveway, I stopped. "What? Whose truck is next to your car?"

Earl tugged on my arm. "There's your daddy's new truck. The dealer called right after we got home to see whether he should drop it off. I told him to bring it by the house. He left a few minutes ago while you were watering the sunflowers. Another friend picked him up. Your daddy had signed all the documents, which means he's the proud owner of a new extended cab pickup."

The black and shiny pickup captured the moon's glow. "Is this really Daddy's?"

"Yes, I'm sure you could drive it until Max gets home. You don't have a vehicle, remember?"

"So, you keep reminding me. I'm fully aware that my car is missing."

"I'd say it's stolen, and you'll probably never see it again."

"I never liked that car, but I finally paid off the loan last year."

"Catch." Earl tossed me the keys, which I promptly dropped. I bent over, grabbing them as if I'd caught a catfish on the line.

My gut rolled with questions about the letter Earl sent me, which opened the tackle box of questions hiding within me. "I'm having trouble understanding why no one told me about Daddy's lung cancer until last week. You've raised me alongside Daddy. We never kept secrets. How could you not tell me?"

Earl opened the driver's door on the new pickup. "Max promised he'd tell you, and then he changed his mind, month after month. Finally, when I noticed his health deteriorating, I had to let you know. I do regret keeping this from you."

I climbed into the seat, the dashboard like a computer, and I fumbled to move closer to the steering wheel so that I could touch the gas pedal. Putting my hands at ten and two, I absorbed the smell of leather. "This is so nice. Daddy's going to love this truck. But I shouldn't be driving it. He should drive it first."

"You have to report for work at the *Tribune* tomorrow, so having a vehicle will help get you there and get you home."

"You're right. I'll be careful. And drive slow."

"This truck has power. At least go the speed limit."

I hopped from the truck. "I'll leave it here for now until I head to the newspaper office in the morning. After that, I'll need to get my driver's license replaced, too, and I didn't cancel my debit card either."

"Yes, take care of business tomorrow. And ride like a champ. Do park the pickup at your house, but take it for a spin first."

"We have dirt and gravel in the driveway; the tires will get dirty."

"They'll get dirty when you drive on the road, so don't try to keep them clean. Life's messy. And trucks get dirty."

I whimpered, "Earl, Daddy will love this truck."

"Oh, but Sally, he loves you being home even more."

Ruby charged up the driveway from the shadows as if she had eavesdropped. "So, you're going to keep the truck? Seriously, Max is in the hospital, and now you're talking about a new truck like it's nothing. And you're going to drive his truck? I can't believe you."

I hollered, "I thought you were gone."

"Seth wasn't home, and his grandmother has the flu. She's not fond of me, so I'm not staying there. She probably doesn't even have the flu. I'll stay on the back porch, if you don't mind."

I hugged her neck as if two sisters were making up. "Yes, stay, please. I don't want to be alone. And this truck means nothing, except that it belongs to Daddy. That makes it special."

Ruby pulled away. "He will like it. But no more hugging. Do not hug me without permission."

Earl reached for Ruby's hand. "You're welcome at either house. Any time."

"Thank you. I'm staying with Sally, but only if she won't hit me or push me or hug me."

I jingled my keys. "No promises, but I do promise I have ice cream."

After I moved the truck into the driveway, I shuffled into the living room with Ruby behind me. I let out a long breath, my energy spent, my legs like noodles, and my tummy craving a giant bowl of ice cream. "Let's check the freezer. Daddy must have vanilla ice cream."

"Yes, ice cream makes life better."

The freezer was packed full of packages of frozen berries and peas and other containers, but not one tub of ice cream. "Does Daddy still have a deep freeze in the shop?"

"Yes, but I'm sure it's full of frozen meat and vegetables. No need to check there." She jumped in front of the doorway leading to the porch. "Why don't we find something else to eat?"

I squinted my eyes as a detective might in a TV show. "Ruby, what are you hiding in the shop?"

"Hiding, what makes you say I'd hide something in the shop?" She inched backward, turning and charging outside, the screen door bouncing in my face.

I rushed with her, not sure where my sudden burst of energy came from, except it must be adrenaline. "Ruby Nell, what are you hiding?"

She darted to the back of the house and rushed to the shop, where she guarded the entry next to the automated garage door. She raised her voice. "There's nothing inside this building except for more jam, and storage stuff, and a freezer full of frozen food."

"So now you're shouting like I'm deaf, and I'm right in front of you. Move out of the way."

"No, we don't need ice cream." Her pitch was higher, as if she could sing soprano in a choir. "Please, don't go inside there."

"Ruby, what are you protecting?"

"It's Seth. He came back with me from his grandma's house."

"What? Where does she live? You came back pretty fast."

"She rents a duplex about three blocks from here. And Seth's not a bad guy. He's trying to put his bad decisions behind him."

"So, is he inside the shop?"

Ruby dropped her arms. "Well, I'm not sure."

133

Shop for Truth

I flipped the light on, marching into the metal building, my heart swimming with memories after seeing Daddy's fishing boat. I glanced around the garage, and there was no Seth. "Ruby? What's with blocking the door if no one's in here?"

She cawed like a bird on a limb. "Sorry, just playing around with you."

I ignored her and disappeared to the lake of memories as I touched the side of the boat. "Daddy's fished from these two seats for as long as I can remember, as far back as my high school days. I sat in one spot journaling or reading, and he in the other holding a fishing pole, trying to snag the big one."

Rube added, "I like to fish. It's peaceful on the water."

"It is peaceful, but fish stink." I pointed to the shiny motor. "Looks like he bought another new putter to get around. He's gone through a few."

"He used his jam money to buy that last year."

Across the oversized garage, jars and jars of jam layered the shelves in the rear. They were labeled and ready to sell. "Since Daddy had all these in stock, why the hurry to label the new batch in the house?"

"Your dad's picked up Earl's traits. He believes you should have replacement jam on the shelf, ready for surprise orders and new customers. Those two men like things in order. Also, Max spent weeks teaching me how to make his perfect jam, too. To pass on the recipe."

"Daddy taught you how to make jam?"

"Uh, yeah, he wanted to pass on the know-how to someone." Ruby squinted, her words softer than the digs she's made when trying to top me in the daughter department, almost as if she wished to take back her last words.

I took a deep breath, remembering the times Daddy asked me to stay, to learn, and see how to make the jam. And again, regret seeped into my heart like a pound of sugar mixing with a gallon of bitter strawberries. "I used to lick his spoon, but I never learned to make jam. I regret it so much."

Ruby touched her nose, wiping a tear that slipped down her face.

I called, "Hey, Seth, are you here? I'm pretty sure Ruby gave you time to escape." My way of changing the subject became ineffective, and all I could think of was how much I've missed my daddy.

Ruby touched the rim of the camouflage boat. "When I went fishing with Max, we often caught a mess of catfish and bass. Stinky they are, but a tasty goodness shows up when you deep fry those babies." She licked her lips.

"I don't fish. I watch people fish."

"Everyone should go fishing." Ruby muddled toward the freezer near the shelves, where stewed tomatoes sat next to the jam.

I pulled on Ruby's arm. "So, where is Seth? I've got a suspicion your tackle box of secrets is holding a wormy part to this story."

Ruby glanced around the room, her gaze stopping on the open window above the freezer. "Seth left by the window."

"I see. So, a quick escape from a redhead, and he's all clear." I turned to Ruby, knowing my part in our friendship held muddy and caked steps, but I tossed the responsibility to her. "Ruby, this has to stop. I know we met last week, and the rocky beginning hasn't improved much, but tell me this: Was Seth's grandma sick when you went over there tonight?"

Ruby climbed into the boat, sitting on the seat, and she wiped the sweat from her brow. Her tone soured. "No, I never knocked on her door."

"So, she doesn't have the flu? And you made the whole story up?"

"Maybe. I haven't talked to Seth's granny tonight."

"What's with your constant lies to me? It makes it hard for me to know how to react or what to do with what you say. It's not helping me trust you around my daddy either. You don't want me mad, but then you do this."

"I'm good with your dad. I've told you. I treat him better than anyone."

I countered, "You're not better to him than Earl."

"Well, I'm better to him than you."

"Are we going to do this again? The constant digs are wearing me out. And your rude comments must end."

"You own part of this. I'm not the only one with the smart-aleck remarks. You have an entire lake full of them. And you're draining the lake on me from your spillway of hate."

"Stop. Daddy would ask us to make up. Besides, the truth wins even if it hurts. We have to start fresh somehow; let's make it now." My mind wavered between reasoning with Ruby and tossing her out on the street. But then Daddy never gives up on people, and I can learn from that, as Earl has told me.

Ruby wiggled in her seat, and I swung a leg up, pulling myself to the spot across from her. It's as if I held a mirror to myself in Ruby. She's a woman with a past who loves Daddy. And I'm a woman with a past, and I, too, love Daddy.

Ruby gave me her take on things. "You're fumbling around with life and wasting time with nonsense. It's time to make the most of the day. And face reality."

I shook my head. "So, you're tossing the fishing line back to me?"

Ruby looked over her shoulder, checking out the room as if she wondered who I might be talking to besides her. She cackled, "Oh, were you talking to yourself or me?"

"What? Of course, I was talking to you. Why would any of what I've said apply to me?"

Ruby extended her arms on each side as if she rowed a boat with oars, waving her arms. "Our boat is in deep water now. Those questions sounded like you've rehearsed them. But if you point all fingers at me, then your life remains the same. I'm not the only person who has issues. You do, too."

The anger sailed up my throat like heartburn, stinging my nasal cavity. "Ruby Nell. This is absolutely the meanest thing to say. This conversation is about you."

Ruby stood up in the boat. "Don't rock the boat, Sally Snow. Or you might have to face your demons."

I rose to my feet, ready to shove Ruby to the concrete floor. "Why can't we have a civil conversation? And why do we have all these layers, which are simply distractions?"

Ruby plopped down, folding her arms. "You want the truth. Fine. I ran into Seth by the pavilion. He was so proud to have a job at the Dusty West Cafe. And he wasn't at his grandma's house tonight. He was dancing under the pavilion downtown like someone whose life is changing, in a good way. He screamed like a madman, a happy one too."

"So, Seth is a little scary?" I dug in, hoping to catch her off guard with another piece of a lie or a twisted retelling of her downtown outing.

"He's a little bit of everything, and he's working on his self-control. His explosion of joy happened as I came past the chamber building. At first, I thought he might be drunk, but he wasn't under the influence. He was happy. That's all. Good old-fashioned happy."

Ruby caught me off guard, and I wasn't sure if she added a new layer to our already long series of storytelling. I played along. "The cafe is where my daddy cooked for a thousand years."

"It hasn't been open that long."

"He loved working there. He wore his white chef hat and created specialties in the kitchen, those people would die for."

"Well, that's what Seth is doing now. He has a range of recipes that your dad passed along. Seth loves to bake and try out new dishes, and his grandma has shown him some of her favorites, too."

"Seth's a cook?"

"Yes, he is a bona fide cook."

"So, Seth was here too, right?"

Ruby rubbed her eyes, the bruise on her head shining a deep blue. "Yes, I let him inside. The keys are under the flowerpot on the back steps, one to the house and one to the shop. He planned to box up the jams by flavor in advance of Pioneer Days. Unfortunately, his new schedule might keep him from helping Max out this year."

"Then why hide?"

"You scare him. And he regrets how he spoke to me in the yard the other night in front of you. He figures you've sized him up. So, I told him to hurry, to load the crates. That I'd distract you."

"Sneaking around isn't a good idea. I do live here. Well, I live here for now." I licked my lips; the salt of dry sweat mingled with the news. "Ruby, our conversations are tough to follow. Simple would help. And truthfulness would be good too."

"But you tend to overreact."

I sighed. "So, when I didn't let the ice cream search end, you were afraid I'd think Seth was trespassing."

Ruby shrugged her shoulders. "Would you have?"

"Yes, I'm sure of it." I reached out with my hand. "Shake with me."

"Shake?"

"Let's shake on it. That we'll be honest with each other."

"I'm not into touching, remember."

I pulled my hand to my side. "You've held my hand already, so what's the big deal?"

"It's got to be my idea."

"Fine, but let's do better. If for no reason, but Daddy."

"You keep saying that, but maybe we need to do this because we're changing our behavior."

I put my hands to my ears. *Whoa!* "That was profound."

Ruby shook her shoulders. "I do have my moments."

I jumped from the boat to the freezer. "So, are we having ice cream or not?"

"Sure, if you want to, but it's late. Sally, you're like a light switch, on and off, and unpredictable."

I grinned. "You should know what unpredictable is like, right?"

Ruby bailed from the boat, too. "Whatever. Come on, Max hides his treats out here, but it's no secret. Earl and I know Max never lets ice cream run out."

I gazed inside the freezer. "Look in here. Who keeps ten gallons of vanilla ice cream?"

"Your daddy does." Ruby came up beside me. "He bought them for whenever you might finally come home. He was always looking for his girl, which is you. I was simply a fill-in, but don't worry, I know that now."

"Boy, I'm a rotten daughter. And you're no fill-in, as you say. God sent you along to comfort my daddy's heart. I'm sorry for lashing out at you all week. You've reminded me of the relationship I've allowed to slip away. It's great to come home."

Ruby raised her eyebrows. "You have a strange way of showing how happy you are to be in New Boston."

"I can be hard to read."

"No kidding."

**

I licked my spoon, knowing we could both sleep until noon if given a chance. But tomorrow, I'm reporting for duty at the newspaper at eight o'clock. I should have told Pearson a later time.

"Ruby, this was the best ice cream, and I'm not sure we needed that second bowl."

She nodded, and Ruby stretched out on the floor with her back up against the couch, and she placed her bowl on the floor. "Ice cream makes me sleepy. Hey, hand me that pen over there and a piece of your dad's airplane paper. I'm in the mood to sketch you."

"What? Me?"

"Yes, hold that smile."

Ruby scribbled on the paper, smirking and nodding. "There you are. See, your smile is back."

"Goodness, it's just my teeth. Don't I get a face?"

"That comes in time." Ruby giggled, folding the paper into an airplane and sending it sailing across the room.

I smiled. "Having a new friend can be like vanilla ice cream, shockingly cold at first but yummy once you digest a few scoops." I placed my bowl on the end table. "Hey, if you want, you can sleep in Daddy's bed. He won't mind. Honest."

"No, the cot on the porch is good enough for me. As I've said, I'm not sleeping in Max's bed."

Ring-a-ling. Ring-a ling.

My heart pounded, my feet racing, and I grabbed the phone in the dining room. "Hello. Yes, I'm Sally."

The voice on the other end pulled me underground, the suffocation of sorrow pouring over me like a boat capsizing in the ripples of a terrible storm. "No! I'll be right there. You must be wrong. Not my daddy!"

Pam Kumpe

Freckles on the Playground

A plump man with earbuds bumped my shoulder, pushing me forward. "Excuse me. I'm counting steps. I'm getting in shape." He kept going, his world full of sunshine and goals.

"Sorry." I left the trail at Tapp Park and crossed to the spot where I once played on the slides. I climbed the metal fort to the top, squeezing inside, bending, unable to stand, only able to sit.

On Saturdays as a girl, after fishing, we'd detour to the park for a few minutes, where I'd wave to my daddy from the fort and where he'd blow a kiss to me.

More than once, he said, "Sunflower, I just blew you another freckle. That's why you have so many, one for each kiss I've sent to you."

I went down the slide, shuffling to the other side of the park to the swing set, holding the chain, sitting down in the rubber seat, pushing myself higher and higher until my hair sailed across my face the wrong way and back again. A hand on my back sent me higher, and I sang, "Go higher, Daddy. Push me to the moon and back to where purple skies and pink clouds meet."

"Yes, Sunflower, the world is yours. Make a difference. Be brave. Be ready to pray. To dream. But always dare to show kindness to others."

"I will. I want to be like you, Daddy."

Dragging my shoes, I slowed the swing, peeking behind me, the shadow of my childhood an imprint on my life, a moment where my daddy showed me who I could become.

Sauntering to the picnic table, I faced the playground where a small girl with red hair and purple sandals picked a wildflower, a yellow one, and she put it in her hair. She twirled around, dancing, her blue top swinging and her smile stretching longer than an ocean wave on a seashore.

She climbed the ladder to the same fort, waving at her father below, who instructed, "Be careful. Forts are great places to go. But to find the miracle, you must venture out to the land below. So come down the slide, and I'll catch you."

The girl yelled, "I'm coming. Catch me."

"Always."

The daisy-like flower slipped from the girl's wavy red locks and floated in the breeze, settling on the grass by my purple tennis shoes.

"I'll be back, Daddy. Got to get my flower."

The girl of about seven jumped to the slide, slipping down the slope, and she fell into her daddy's arms, only to run over to me. She paused, gazing at me, her freckles a reflection of how love floated into her life.

The girl's grin revealed a missing tooth, and she said, "Hi, you look sad." She picked up the daisy and placed it in my hand. "Put this flower in your hair. It will make you happier."

"Thank you." I tucked the bloom into my hair like a barrette, the breeze sending me to my feet. "What's your name?"

"I'm Daisy."

I followed the girl to the ladder, to the makeshift bridge with flat metal links connecting the platform, to another ladder leading to the fort. At the bridge, she turned back to me. "You've gone this way before. It's time to take the other path."

143

Her wisdom and words sounded more like those of an adult than those of a small child. I begged, "But I want to go with you. We can sing and pretend to conquer the aliens hiding in the oak trees."

"Not today. Today you must take the road less traveled, the one you've avoided all your life."

"Wait, I know you. And those green eyes. The red hair. But your words are wiser than mine. Your name isn't Daisy."

She swung sideways, holding onto the ropes on the bridge, wiggling for balance. "I speak for my daddy. He's taught me so much. To climb. To swing. To play. Even to pray. And, to hold on. But sometimes you must let go."

"But where is the road I must take? I don't know what to do with my life."

"Look for the sunflowers, and all the lost daisies, because Daddy says they are the windows which show you the way."

"I've got to say goodbye to my daddy at three. His funeral's today."

The girl pointed to the shade tree. "Daddy, wave to her. Let her know you're happy. Let her know the sunflowers bloom forever in heaven."

I glanced over the platform's railing to the girl's father, who now looked like my daddy. He was standing taller. His smile was huge. And he blew me a kiss. "One more freckle for my girl. Daddy's been looking for you. And there you are."

I collapsed to my knees, holding my face, catching the freckle. "Daddy, don't go. Don't go. Over the last three days, I've been at a loss; the ache is more than my heart can withstand. I can't take this sorrow."

From the shade, a breeze placed words in my heart. "Sunflower, I'm with the Father. All is well."

**

Ruby's voice invaded my world. "What are you doing? I've driven all over town looking for you. We have minutes to get to the funeral home. They sent a limo to the house to pick you up, but you weren't in your room."

I ran my fingers through my hair, the yellow flower floating to my feet. "I was daydreaming and taking a walk. I told you I never planned to ride in the limo. I'm driving Daddy's truck."

"Well, that's perfect. You didn't change clothes either. You're still wearing your jeans and tennis shoes. It's too late to go home to change. Let's go. The truck's right there." Ruby pointed to the parking lot across from the ball fields.

"You have a key to my daddy's truck?"

"No, you're like him. You leave keys everywhere."

I sat on the top of the ladder. "Ruby, did you know you're parked where there used to be a public pool?"

"I kind of remember."

"I swam there when I was in elementary school. Daddy would drop me off, but one time he stayed, wearing his flannel shirt and straw hat so he wouldn't get sunburned. The lifeguard didn't notice the boy in the deep end who was sinking."

"Did the kid drown?"

"No, Daddy dove into the pool and rescued the boy. He was right where he was supposed to be, flannel and all."

"Your dad was the kind of person whom God has used to touch lives."

"Another time, Daddy taught the Bible lesson at Kids Beach Club, and he witnessed children learning about God. He loved being a part of that ministry."

"I've heard of how much that program has done, and they meet right after school with the children every Tuesday with different Bible stories, songs, and object lessons."

"Daddy was so involved in the community. He loved going to the homeless shelter too, back when he was younger." I sniffled. "I'm going to miss him so much. I already do."

Ruby motioned for me to come down. "We have to go. It's almost time for the funeral. I can't believe we've gone through so much already, having just met. We've endured misunderstandings, rattlesnakes, hospital trips for stitches and bandages, and enjoyed ice cream with each other, and had so many arguments."

"We have taken a ride on a roller coaster."

"Yes, so much in such a short time. And to think, we have bruises on our foreheads, and we're both rather stubborn."

"I'm not as stubborn as you."

Ruby wiped a tear. "Don't start with me. I'm barely keeping it together. I'm trying to figure out what my next move is after today. But first, we have a funeral to attend. And I must make Max proud of me."

I took in her words. "Yes, I've got to stop the madness and make my daddy proud, too. I used to dream of a sister when I was younger, especially at night when I'd get scared. I longed to have someone climb up the fort so we could shoot our pinecones at the aliens. An alien melts if a pinecone hits it."

Ruby smiled. "You have the strangest imagination."

"I am a writer." I giggled, my love for stories arising from the deep well within me. "I sure could use a hug right now; wait, you're not into touching."

"It depends." Ruby stood on the first step of the rung and bolted up the ladder to the first layer of the gym platform, plopping next to me. "I could use a hug today if you don't mind."

"I don't mind at all." I wrapped my octopus' arms around Ruby, and I melted into the embrace of someone who knew my daddy's kindness firsthand.

Ruby yanked free. "That's enough hugging. You can't be late for your daddy's funeral."

"True, let's go. But I'm driving."

"No, I drove here, and I have the keys."

"It's my truck."

"Technically, it's not yours. The truck belongs to Max."

"Stop it."

Ruby dangled the key bob in the air. "I hope there's not a rattlesnake on this ride." Her cackle sent the birds flying from a nearby tree as we rushed like wanna-be track stars across the park to the parking lot.

I hopped into the driver's seat, leaving the door open. "Give me the keys, or I'll make you late."

"We're already late. Max is presiding over the funeral. You'll have to deal with him."

"Fine. I'll walk."

"Stop acting like a child."

"You're a fine one to give me advice."

A black truck sped into the parking lot, and the wavy-haired driver rolled the window down as he made a turn facing us. Pearson shook his head, the tension in his brow obvious from the wrinkles above his brow. "Ladies, come on. I've been sent on a mission to find you. Everyone's waiting."

We hopped into the truck, me on the passenger side and Ruby behind the wheel. She drove behind Pearson down Sunset, heading to the funeral home on Highway 8 near my home church, First Baptist. "Ruby, maybe we could go to church together soon."

Ruby gripped the wheel. "Maybe, we'll see. I might be moving away. I've called my auntie. She was thrilled to hear from me. A change might be good for me."

"What? Stay here with me. At my house. No need to make a hurried decision."

**

We were met at the door by an usher who sent us to the right, to a small chapel. Ruby and I were escorted into the room and seated in the first row. I looked back, and Pearson sat down, disappearing into the crowd. I took in the faces of those who knew my daddy, and it's as if a story rested inside each person who sat inside the chapel.

Ronny Riggs, a friend of my daddy, once helped a woman who sat downtown with her dog and two rabbits. Ronny paid to fix her car, made sure she had food, and put her up in a hotel room for four nights.

Behind Ronny sat a gray-haired woman who once owned the flower shop. She wept, sniffling. The bald man next to her wrapped an arm around her shoulder, consoling her.

I folded my hands, the sweat pouring from my palms and from behind my ears. I tapped my foot, and my knee bounced. Ruby whispered, "Stop wiggling."

"I can't help it."

The coffin with my daddy held a spray of sunflowers, glorious yellow-and-gold mixes, beautiful colors for his farewell celebration. I'd requested the coffin be closed, having said my goodbyes to Daddy yesterday in private.

I held the program, with a picture of praying hands on the front and the funeral order listed inside. With what seemed like fifty organs playing, the music to "I'll Fly Away" floated into the chapel like a sweet breeze.

Earl came near the pulpit, standing off to the side, clutching his Bible. He waited for the song's final chorus and winked at me the way he used to when I'd show him my report card as a girl. A wink of approval. A moment of friendship. Not only to Daddy, but to me.

Earl broke the silence that lingered after the song. "Good afternoon, we're here to say farewell to a dear friend, Max Williams."

Now both feet were tapping, and I started to run from the building. Ruby placed her arm around my shoulder. "Stay. Don't panic."

I turned to her ear. "I thought you didn't like touching other people."

"If I instigate it, then touching is allowed."

Earl gave details, beginning with Daddy's birth, through his contributions to town, to his love for sunflowers and ice cream, and, of course, his cooking and the way he stocked all the refrigerators in town with his jam.

Earl added, "His greatest love was for his daughter, Sally Marilyn Williams Snow; he simply called her Sunflower."

I wept, the tears falling from a place where memories captured my joy like a jar of jam, tasty and good.

Earl went on. "Let me tell you about the time when Max taught Sally a lesson about strangers."

My stomach churned; a shot like ruined milk coated my mouth from the back of my throat, strangling me. I popped, racing down the center aisle. "No, I can't do this. I can't say goodbye to my daddy."

I stormed from the chapel out the front door and ran to the truck, sitting on the bumper, my eyes burning with years of regret.

Pam Kumpe

Astonished Joy

"Sally, where are you? Stop hiding. Now's the time to honor your father." Earl's voice carried over the parking lot like a mallard duck in flight, and the summons for me to answer rose louder than his usual tone. "Sally, please, where are you?'

I stood up. "I'm right here." I sniffled, wiping any mascara from my eyes to the back of my hand.

"Can I convince you to come back inside so we can hold your dad's funeral?"

"Earl, I'm not even forty, and I've buried my son and my husband and now my daddy."

"Sally, sometimes we don't have answers for tragedies or illness, especially for loss. But that's when we run to God and cast our cares on Him. Remember, God is compassionate and knows your sorrow. There's even a short verse that talks about a time when Jesus cried."

"A short verse?" I paced between the cars, which were lined up in rows behind each other, those ready to drive to the cemetery.

Earl paced with me, one car row to my right. "It simply says, Jesus wept."

"He wept?" The fog in my mind kept me from focusing on what Earl said to me.

"Yes, Jesus wept. And will you please stop pacing? Stand still. Please."

"I'm having trouble staying put." I raised my arms like a flapping duck. "And why in the world would Jesus cry?"

Earl faced me on the other side of the blue car. "He cried after speaking to Mary and Martha because their brother Lazarus had died."

"But Earl, I know that story, and Jesus ended up raising Lazarus from the dead. Their sorrow went from weeping to astonished joy."

"But that's the astonishing joy we can have in knowing your dad is with Jesus in heaven."

"Earl, you've gone and started preaching."

"Well, Sally, I've pastored for more than thirty years. I believe good preaching keeps us grounded. When did you last open your Bible or lean on God for help? Why are you trying to deal with your sorrow alone?"

"I have no idea where my Bible is. It's probably in storage." I charged around the car, gazing into his eyes. "I want to trust God with my pain, but it's hard. Lately, it seems I've lost hope, and it's miles away."

"You're in the middle of the storm. And it takes effort to fight your way toward life."

"Earl, I don't have the strength. It feels like morning, but I'm fast asleep. Everything's more than I can hold."

"Then fall into God's arms." Earl reached for me, embracing me with a lifetime of love, and his whisper healed my soul. "Sunflower, you'll always be your daddy's girl. When Minnie passed away, I cried on my pillow for her. Let your tears fall. Take what's left in you and whatever's worth holding onto, embrace it."

"I'm a prisoner in my skin. And you see how I am on my own."

"I'll be next door. I'll water the sunflowers and the garden if you need me to when it's too hard to turn on the faucet."

"Thank you, Earl." I sobbed, my heart hoping to reawaken.

"Don't forget, we have hope in seeing our families again. Your dad is waiting in heaven. And he's not sick anymore."

I sighed, my heart sensing a melody of hope at having such a great daddy.

Earl wrapped his arm around my shoulders. "Let's go inside. I'll walk with you. Your dad has friends who want to say goodbye to him."

"Yes, sir. I'll come with you. But let me go inside at my own pace."

Inside, I took my seat up front, with Earl moving to his place, and the chatter of questions and remarks gave way to silence. "Sorry, folks, let's begin this celebration again. Friends, I want to tell you of a time when Max taught Sally about the meaning of who is a stranger and what to do if you see one."

I smiled, remembering the retelling of this story, but not genuinely remembering it, since I was four years old when Daddy saw me getting too close to the road. The fruit-man, Mr. Shuker, pulled up in his old truck, and he handed me an apple from a crate, which I gobbled down.

Later, Daddy said, "Sally, you're getting too close to the street. If a stranger comes, don't talk to them and run inside the house. I need you to be safe."

The next day, as I played in the yard beside the Mimosa, a mere shade tree back then, I raced into the living room, screaming at my daddy. "There's a stranger in the yard. He's coming after me."

Daddy held my hand and marched to the front porch. He chuckled, "Sally, that's no stranger. That's Earl."

Earl brought me to the present with his words, and because Ruby nudged me. "Pay attention."

I wrinkled my nose at her. "I am."

Earl made eye contact with me, ending one of many stories he'd share about Daddy. "Sally was afraid of me for a few weeks after that, and every time I walked outside, she yelled, 'Stranger danger.' And I responded, not a stranger, so no danger."

Ruby leaned in closer. "Your daddy must have laughed so hard at you when you were growing up."

I kept my voice low. "He laughed when sad or mad and said he chose not to let circumstances determine his outlook."

Ruby bumped me with her shoulder. "You could learn from him."

I pursed my lips like a ventriloquist. "And you could too."

Earl slapped the pulpit top. "Funny thing is, the next time Mr. Shuker drove by, Sally wouldn't leave the porch. She was afraid of everyone for the next couple of years. He offered her pears, apples, and strawberries. And she never budged."

The rest of the funeral swirled into fast-paced, like someone hit the forward button on a remote, only to hit pause with some slow-singing and sad hymns. Finally, after more goodbyes at the gravesite, everyone's leaving the Red Bayou Cemetery. It's hard to believe that a week prior, Daddy and I held a birthday party for my mom here, and now he's buried next to her.

I waved to Ruby across the fence. "Ride with Earl; I'll be fine. I'll come home in a little while."

"But there's food at the house—lots of it. The covered dishes are sitting on top of the jam on the table. What do we need to do?"

"Eat what you want. Freeze what you don't want. And save me a plate for later."

**

I ran my fingers over the top of my mom's tombstone and then stared at the pile of dirt next to her marker, a relatively small spot for my daddy. He had lived quietly on Front Street, taking grand steps for God without ribbons, trophies, or titles.

I'd watched the cemetery workers lower Daddy's coffin, and when it wobbled, I corrected them. "Don't drop my daddy."

The three men never responded to me, which probably saved them from my wrath. So now I'm sitting in the dirt between my parents and holding onto what's left of me. My heart is dripping with a cold ache inside my chest. And I'm thinking of all the things I never said to my daddy and those I never had the chance to tell my mom.

I spoke to God. "I'm getting tired, and I need somewhere to begin. What do I do now?"

A voice responded from near the old frame church. "Begin with a step."

I raised my head, trying to see if the workers were close, but there was no sign of them. The wind whipped through the brown leaves on the towering oak trees in the parking area. "Hello, who's there?"

From behind a tree, a voice answered, "You have miles of memories; let them carry you. On gray days, don't sway. On blue days, don't forget how your daddy loved you. You're never alone."

"Who are you? Show yourself."

"It's not for me to show; it's for you to know there's hope beyond the grave. Your daddy and your mom belonged to the family."

I interrupted. "What family? What do you mean?"

"The family of God. The Lord called them his children. And you are His, too. The Father is looking for you. It's time to wake up, to stand with all that you have left. Find your strength and go write your story."

I ran to a tree, then another, and finally to another, trying to find the voice singing hope to me, a voice which sounded familiar but spoke with odd phrasing. "Where are you? Who's there?"

At the white-framed church, the double doors flew open, slamming against the frame.

"Wait, who's there?"

I charged inside the sanctuary between two small rows of pews and found myself facing a cross on the wall behind the pulpit. I spun around. "Hey, is anyone here?"

From behind me, the voice answered. "I'm here. It's time for you to take that job. You first said no. And then you said yes. With your father's passing, I understood another no. But take a few days and come see me."

The face of my high school debate team friend held a camera.

"Pearson? What are you doing?"

"We all need friends. Ruby asked me to stay behind and make sure that you get home safely. And then you were talking to yourself, and I decided to answer."

"I was talking to God. But I feel like I'm losing my mind. My furniture is in storage, and my friend in Dallas has my cockatiel. My life is also in Dallas. So why would I stay in New Boston?"

"Because your life is here now. And this is home. Earl said you found your smile when you got here, except when you were arguing with Ruby."

I grinned. "She tests me."

"What you're finding is your way. Earl sent you a letter because it was time to come back home for your daddy. So be here now because this is where you belong."

155

I put my face into my hands, the tears falling, my knees wobbling. I muttered, "I'm tired of the old me."

"The one I remember from high school is the fiery one I see when you're around Ruby. She makes your red hair shine."

I touched my ponytail. "She's a bit much. I may need to tone her down some."

Pearson moved closer, and I sobbed, snot running down my chin. "I can use a friend. And I will need that job."

"Fine, friends are good for the heart. You'll have time to write the piece for our Pioneer Day insert, too, so that the chamber can award the prize the following weekend after the festival."

"So did you wait behind just to make sure I took your reporter job?"

Pearson handed me the camera. "Well, you tell me."

I wrapped my fingers around the Canon, and for the first time, I saw Pearson's green eyes. And the dimple on his left cheek.

Pearson interrupted my staring at him. "Let me follow you to the house. My truck is parked next to yours."

Messy Chimney Falls

I climbed from the truck at the house, and Pearson waved from the road, not stopping, and drove on. Ruby ran to me. "You can't believe what we've dealt with since we got here."

"What are you yelling about?"

She danced around me. "So, Pearson did follow you home?"

"Don't act so surprised. He told me you asked him to stay." I reached for the strap on the Canon as the camera fell from my shoulder.

"So, you do have the camera. Does that mean you also have a job?"

"I have the most conniving friends surrounding me; you, Earl, and Pearson meddle in my life. And yes, I have a job. I start this Friday."

"Friends? So, we're friends?"

"Sure, but what are you dealing with inside the house?"

"Just don't get mad."

"Why would I get mad?"

"It's a mess."

We marched into the house. "What in the world happened in here?"

"Earl and I came inside to eat, and when we got here, a mallard duck attacked us, flying from beneath the kitchen table."

"Wait, a duck? In this house?"

"Yes, he was flapping and clucking and making a mess in the front room and even the dining room, and he pooped all over your bed."

"How did he get inside? It's August. He should be at a lake. Not here in town."

"Well, he might have been lost. Earl's outside, and he lassoed him, sort of. But the duck got tangled in the rope, and we think the duck might have a broken leg."

"Are you serious?" I didn't wait for her answer. "Look, the couch is covered in soot. The pillows will need deep scrubbing. And what is all over the floor in the dining room?"

"He got into the casseroles and desserts and ate complete platefuls of some dishes. I have no idea what he devoured. He must have been hungry."

"The poor duck was scared, that's all, and he didn't know how to get out of the house."

Earl stepped in from the kitchen. "I'm taking the duck to Dr. Mender. Maybe he can fix the poor thing. I found a cat carrier out in the shop and pushed the duck inside. He's in the backseat of my car. I'll be back."

I stopped Earl and stepped toward him. "But Earl, how did a duck get in here?"

"Check the tracks. You'll find out by backtracking his prints. Oh, and Snowball and Charcoal must have chased him, too. Someone left the cats in the house. Between the three of them, the lamp got knocked over. And a few jars of jam. The cats are going to need baths, too."

The new disaster overwhelmed my ability to cope. "Ruby, will it get any easier?"

"Will what?"

"Will it get easier to come inside this house without seeing my daddy?"

Ruby took my hand. "I see your daddy. He sat in the recliner, drinking sweet tea, and napped there since I've known him. I see him at the stove, tasting his jam, and in the yard watering his garden. And I see him flying paper airplanes. And writing you letters. I never want to forget any of those moments."

I bent down to track some prints, which led me to the fireplace by the front door. "The chimney is full of a fresh layer of ashes. That blasted duck fell into the house from the roof."

"Do you think so? Earl mentioned it, but I don't see a duck losing its balance and tumbling down a chimney."

I laughed. "Look, if God can get me home, then He can send a duck into our midst."

"Goodness, now you're saying God is using a duck?"

"I don't know. Maybe."

"Well, Earl is good at fixing things. So maybe helping the duck will make him feel useful."

Ruby argued. "And we get to clean up this mess?"

"I'm too tired to know. I just know my life has been a mess, and I've flown into places as if I had tumbled down a chimney. I've lost my balance by letting my sorrow destroy my living. Maybe this is a picture of my life."

Ruby knelt, looking up the chimney. "I've flown down a few chimneys myself." She reached upward, only for a bucket of soot to pour onto her head, sending a cloud of gray into the living room. *Whoa!* "I didn't mean to make this worse."

"Ruby, it's time we clean up what we can."

"Are you talking about the house or our lives?"

I smiled. "Both."

For the next bit, we sat in soot, crying like schoolgirls, knowing full well the rest of the evening meant soap and water and scrubbing would follow. Those to clean the house. And those to clean our attitudes and choices, too.

**

I wiped soot from my nose and stood up. "Ruby, you said something earlier. You said you could see Daddy writing letters to me. I never got any letters. He called from time to time, but nothing in the mail."

"He wrote you a letter off and on, all this year. We would eat ice cream on Friday nights as he watched reruns of John Wayne on the Western channel. That's when he'd write to you."

"No, are you sure?"

"I'm positive. I bought the stamps."

"I've never received one letter." I stomped around, stirring up the ashes. "I don't understand."

"But he did write you those letters. Secret dad-to-daughter stuff, I'm sure."

I tiptoed over the Styrofoam and splattered food, heading for the trash bags. "If he wrote letters, then maybe they're in his room."

"Can I help you look? I don't want you screaming at me for coming into his bedroom again."

"That was before I knew you or who you were or your intentions." I pulled her arm. "Come on. Let's find them."

Ruby argued, "But shouldn't we clean up this food and the soot?"

"It can wait. Letters are more important."

We barreled into Daddy's room, the bedspread faded from age, and his two pillows were flat like pancakes the way he liked them. "Ruby, anything in the closet? A box or a case?"

"Nothing, just flannel fishing shirts and blue jeans. His chef's hat is on the top shelf. And a shoebox with dress loafers. They look brand new."

I pulled out drawer after drawer in his chest of drawers. "He has more underwear, T-shirts, and tons of socks. But wait, here's an old wallet." I flipped the leather wallet open. "Here's a photo of Daddy with my mom. They were roller skating."

Ruby skated to my side. "Let me see. Oh, she's pretty. Red hair like you. Cute smile too. She looked happy."

"Daddy told me how when they dated, he taught her how to roller skate because she grew up ice skating."

"She could ice skate?"

"She could do anything from the way Daddy talked, except roller skate. Because one time he was skating backward, holding her hands, and he hit a quarter on the floor with his wheel. She tumbled on top of him as they crashed to the floor, breaking Daddy's elbow."

"And he still asked her to marry him?"

"Yeah, that very night."

"He did not. He wouldn't have proposed."

I gazed at the photo. "He did, too. She stayed in the emergency all night with him while he was x-rayed and when they put his arm in a cast. He knew she loved him because she wasn't a night owl, and she held his hand, apologizing."

"Now, isn't that a little mushy?"

"From what I've heard, they could be over the top."

Ruby knelt on the floor. "Hey, there's a storage bin under here."

I pushed her aside. "Let me see."

"Stop the pushing. We've talked about touching me."

"Sorry, I forgot." I yanked on the wooden bin, not much bigger than a tackle box. "Surely we'll find them here."

Ruby and I sat with the box between us, and I lifted the lid. "Here's an old fishing lure. And a copy of an old driver's license. And the deed to the house. And their marriage license."

Ruby reached into the box. "What's this? Could this be your mother's wedding ring?"

I felt the excitement of the surprise. "I bet this is hers. Daddy and Mom wore bands. Simple, gold ones."

Ruby meddled. "Where is your wedding ring?"

I gulped, shamed by knowing what I did with mine. "I couldn't pay the rent and pawned my ring. I planned to go back and get it, but money was too tight."

"Sorry, I asked. I guess that was one of the falling-in-the-chimney moments."

"Yeah, one of many." I slipped the ring on my finger, but my knuckle kept it from going on. "Mom must have had teeny fingers."

"You do have big hands."

"I got those from my dad." I tossed the ring into the box.

Ruby pulled a paper from the bottom of the box. "What's this?"

"Let me see." I snapped the newspaper clipping from Ruby's hand. "Look at this. It's a story about a hero who saved …" I handed her the clipping back.

Ruby cocked her head. "What's wrong?"

"That's a story from the wreck that killed my mom. It happened downtown one night when Daddy dodged some teens racing their cars. When Daddy swerved, our car flipped, pinning my mom inside."

Ruby showed me the photo above the story. "Who in the world shot the picture? He must have been right there when it happened."

"Yeah, it was the local reporter. He was leaving the newspaper office when the accident happened and snapped the photo."

Ruby pointed at the page. "He caught an image of a man carrying a baby. Is that you?"

I grabbed the paper back. "Yes, Fred Collins saved my life." I put my hand to my mouth. "Is he related to you? I'd forgotten his name until now. Are you ...?"

Ruby bit my head off. "Just because we have the same last name doesn't make us related."

"Fine, I was only asking."

Ruby ripped the clipping from my grasp, shoving it into the box.

I pressed her. "From what Earl and Daddy said, Fred died when I was in third grade or somewhere about then."

"Well, I'll tell you why he died." Ruby put her hands on her hips, standing up. "It's because Fred Collins was my dad. So there! We were related. My dad drank himself sick and hurt my mom and me. And yet, there he is in a photo carrying a baby, and it's you."

"I had no idea. Daddy said Fred rescued me, but Mom was trapped. No one got to her in time."

Ruby shouted, "When I was ten, my dad shot himself. We weren't home, but my mom found him. It was horrible. Just horrible."

I reached for Ruby's hand, jumping up, but she yanked it from my grasp. "Don't touch me."

I grabbed her hand again. "I'm not listening to you. Don't you see what's happened?"

"What? What's happened?"

"Your dad saved me. And my daddy saved you."

Ruby crumpled to the floor. "Max loved me. Like a dad should."

I hugged her. "And your dad saved me before our car caught fire."

We huddled together, covered in soot, wrapped in sorrow, and coming to terms with how our childhoods were connected—our stories held horrible images and yet, life-giving chapters of hope.

Pam Kumpe

Write to the Heart

Over the last two days, Ruby and I had scrubbed, mopped, and laundered the sheets and comforters, along with the dish towels and curtains. We wiped every surface in the house too, cleaning up the disaster of a mess left behind by the visiting off-balance duck.

Earl left the invader at the vet, and the doctor believed the free-faller would gain full use of his leg. Earl reminded me that a duck's leg is called a shank when I asked about the duck's injury. Shank. Leg. Either way, the little guy will fly again.

I did shrink the curtains in the living room and dining room, which sent me to Walmart, and the new ones are prettier with brown-and-white stripes. They match the brown couch, especially since I bought a couple of new throws too. My final paycheck arrived yesterday, so my account has a few dollars, and I finally canceled my debit card over the phone. Thankfully, no one had tried to use it.

Ruby did remind me that we have savings accounts at the credit union. But I'm not ready to use Daddy's money.

The cushions on the couch survived by using dish soap, and if I'm not careful, a bubble pops up when I press down on the fabric. But when the cushions are completely dry, the bubbles will disappear. Bubbles seem like my tears; they show up when pressed, but slowly, the tears dry up and give way to happy memories.

Our trash pile on the curb is so high, and I'm sure people driving by think I've tossed out my daddy's stuff. I'm leaving his bedroom intact for now; nothing will go. I still need his things close to me.

Ruby and I've gone through two boxes of trash bags, gathering up food from the floor, and we've wiped down the jars of jam on the table. I only lost a few jars, thankfully.

This afternoon, we scribbled handwritten notes using Daddy's airplane paper, using the stack to fly gratefulness to the friends who thought of me. Who thought of Daddy. Who loved him, too.

I've made sun tea as Daddy would, and checked the mail as Daddy would, and sat in his chair as he would, but so far, in my mind, it's as if he's fishing at the lake and might come in later. Oh, how I'd love to take his boat out and go fishing with my daddy. One more time.

I'm putting on my best face for the world. But this is the most brutal week, and it's taking me right down to my knees. It's not what I want, but the hurt reminds me of love. The love I have for my daddy will carry me through. I wake up at the wee hours of the morning and know the only way to live is to breathe, and I must find purpose and make each second matter. No more running away. No more hiding in the garden.

I fluffed Daddy's pillow, the last of the laundry, finished. The house is ready for life and living and new seasons, but does it get any easier? I hope so. "Ruby, I made macaroni salad if you want some for supper."

She bellowed from the back porch. "Thanks, but I don't like pasta."

"Seriously, you don't eat pasta?"

"No. I've never liked noodles of any kind."

"I have so much to learn about you."

She yelled, "But I know about you. Max kept me informed and compared your life to that of a squirrel."

I marched to the porch where she sat. "A squirrel?"

"Yes, they flit around in the yard, eating nuts from the pecan trees and birdseed from the feeders. They climb trees and jump from limb to limb. But then, when they focus, they sit still and take in their surroundings."

"You're making that up."

"I might be, but you are a squirrel. Flit. Eat. Fill your time with busy work so you won't face your surroundings."

I plopped onto the cot. "How can you sleep here?"

"This cot's home for me. And your daddy made my surroundings safe. And I could rest."

Meow.

Charcoal stretched out next to Ruby, purring.

"I guess he feels safe on this cot, too."

"Yeah, where's Snowball? I haven't seen him around."

"He was gagging in the front yard earlier. I think some of that food he ate has made him sick."

I pressed down. "This cot is hard."

"It's mine."

"It's not long enough."

"It's fine."

"Let's clear it out. You can take my room."

"We've talked about this. I'm not sleeping in the house."

"Why? The bed's softer."

"Sally, let it go. This is my room for now. I'm not sure what's next. I've told you I have some decisions to make."

"And I've told you to stay."

"I have to find a place to call my own. It's like all of this will go away in the blink of an eye. This has been a wonderful dream."

"For me, the last two years have felt like a nightmare."

Ruby wiped her brow, picking up Charcoal, petting him. "Will I ever find somewhere to call my home? It's like when the day breaks, I'm like a river, ready to go. The landscape of my life has changed once more, and some people come and go. But I promise I'll never forget how God graced me with the love of *your* earthly father to remind me of how much I'm loved by God, too."

"You're overthinking this. Just stay."

"You're home. I'm not. I'm just like a squirrel, too. It may be time for me to run toward my life like the river, moving to the place I belong. It's time for me to focus on my surroundings."

"What do you like to do? As I said, I don't know a lot about you."

"In high school, I loved cameras and art."

"Wait, where did you go to high school?"

"Just down the road in Hooks. We moved a lot over the years. But I graduated from Hooks. And I loved watching the journalism students take photographs at football games or shoot photos of different events."

I charged from the porch. "I'll be right back." I reached the dresser, picking up the Canon that Pearson gave me for my reporting, and barreled back to Ruby's side. "Look, take this camera. I'll show you how to use it. One step at a time. I bet Pearson will give you a job too. Come on. I love words. You love photographs. Let's do this."

"Sally, you haven't even asked Pearson."

I paused, remembering how Pearson's eyes held a glint of light the other day at the old church. Maybe I can persuade him to take on two employees. "Look, let me call Pearson. It's worth a try."

"If he says no, I'll understand."

"If he says no, I'll pressure him by telling him I'm not taking the job unless you can come."

"You need a job."

"So do you. We both do."

"You can't bully your way into working for Pearson."

"I can try."

Ruby nudged me. "And the squirrel is back, flitting around and unfocused."

"Hey, I'm focused on your staying and working at the *Tribune*."

We laughed for the first time since the funeral, and I hugged Ruby.

"No touching. Gosh, I have rules."

"I know. And I break them."

I leaned back against the screen wall behind the cot. "Hey, what's in the small trunk by that stack of crates. Is it yours?"

"No, it's been there since I started sleeping here."

I shuffled across the porch. "We've not found Daddy's letters anywhere, and why haven't we looked inside there?"

"I never noticed it or thought about the trunk. Besides, for the past two days, we've stacked all the trash out here in front of it until we lugged the bags to the street." Ruby stood next to me. "Do you think Max hid the letters inside this trunk?"

"I don't know, but we're going to find out." I pulled the metal latch on the trunk, digging inside. "Look, recipes for jam. And recipes for all kinds of desserts. And more recipes for Daddy's favorites, like his Thanksgiving dressing and chocolate cake with cream cheese frosting. Even recipes for how to make homemade biscuits."

Ruby moved me aside when my voice quivered, "Let me look. Here's an old pair of eyeglasses. And a jar of sunflowers. I wonder if they will grow. No telling how long they've been in here."

I pushed her aside. "Letters. We're looking for letters."

Meow. Meow.

Ruby opened the back door, and Snowball scampered in, bending his head, rubbing and twisting his body up next to me. "Sweet kitty. I know you miss Daddy. We all do."

Ruby dug into the trunk. "Hey, here's a folder."

I grabbed it from her. "Let me have it."

"Pushy, aren't we?"

"I can be. I need to read those letters." I opened the flap, and my excitement turned to disappointment. "Just old checking account registers from way back. Maybe he tossed the letters into the trash."

Ruby nodded. "I know you wish you could find them, but you do know how much he loved you?"

"Yes, I know. I'm my daddy's girl."

"What do you think the letters would say that you don't already know?"

"I don't know. It's just that the letters would be from him."

We played with the cats, rubbing their bellies and kissing them on the head. Two cats. Two women. New days ahead. A chance to turn darkness into light.

I jumped to my feet. "I'm watering the garden. The sunflowers still have some life in them."

Ruby ran to the kitchen. "I'm making a fried bologna sandwich."

As I stepped into the yard, I found myself marching to the shop and standing by Daddy's boat. "Daddy, if you saved those letters, where in the world would you have put them?"

Rummaging in between the boxes off to the side and the spider webs, I leaned on the freezer. The heat of the leftover worry of the day landed on me like a bucket of worms from a day of fishing.

I wiped the sweat from my eyes and climbed into the boat, sitting next to Daddy's tackle box, the one I'd given him for Christmas a few years back. "Daddy, let's go fishing. I'd hook up this boat to the truck right now if I knew how. If it would bring you back."

I reached for the tackle box, flipped the latch open, and, on top of bobbles, lures, hooks, and weights, I gazed at a stack of letters addressed to Sally Snow. I screamed, "Daddy, you didn't throw them away!"

Clutching the envelopes, I pressed them to my chest, my heart bursting with a renewed joy at having my daddy's last words in my hands, and ripped the small stack open, taking in the short letters with the longest meanings and reading them.

Dear Sunflower,
I never knew how much I loved your mother until we had you. I loved her ten times more. Keep your mother's photo close. She would be proud of you. Love, Dad

Dear Sunflower,
I never knew what a small girl could do to my heart until you climbed into my lap and kissed my cheek. Your heart is enormous. Use it to love others. Love, Dad

Dear Sunflower,
I never knew a Band-Aid could fix a thousand hurts until you learned to ride your bike. Keep Band-Aids nearby. Keep pedaling into your future. Love, Dad

Dear Sunflower,
Keep Snowball fed. And Charcoal. Pet them, too. Hold them. They need you. You need cats. Rescue those you can. Love, Dad

Dear Sunflower,
In school, you were often alone; use your uniqueness to see those who need friendship. Serve somewhere. Be a friend to the lonely. Love, Dad

Dear Sunflower,
You have given my life joy and heartache, and laughter and pain. Rise above the hard times. Laugh when you can. And know I would pick you from all the babies in the hospital once more. And remember, you're my child. Always. Love, Dad

Dear Sunflower,
I love you. I have ice cream in the freezer. And sweet tea in the fridge. And sunflowers in the garden. Please come home. I don't like the distance between us. Again, please come see me. Love, Dad

My tears dropped like petals from a flower, and each short letter dropped to my feet inside the boat. It's as if I'd caught a mess of fish, and I don't like to fish. But this catch was worth it. Not stinky, one bit.

Daddy's letters were glimpses of light, and I'll treasure his words forever. I whispered, "Daddy, I'm home. I'm going to write a story that will make you proud. You'll see."

Write Ruby's Story

"I'm ready to take on my assignment, but first, I have a request."

Pearson put his hand up. "Sally, you stormed into this newspaper office ten minutes ago, and you're insisting on making demands. Unfortunately, we're short on time, and I've made you a list of people for you to interview. One of those will win the inaugural hero award during the festival, but asking favors from me isn't high on my list. I insist that you get to work, because as you know, it's Friday, and your deadline is Sunday night."

I snapped the list from Pearson's hand. "But first ..."

"No more stalling or excuses."

Waving the paper in the air, I explained, "I don't have any excuses, and the only stalling is coming from you since you're not listening to me. You can help Ruby by giving her a job. She loves cameras, and I've shown her how to use the Canon, well, on automatic. She's a natural and great at framing photos. We practiced last night."

Pearson rubbed his brow, closing the laptop on his desk. "One lesson and she's an expert?"

"No, not an expert, but she's willing to learn. She's outside waiting for you to say yes. I told her you were a reasonable man. One who would jump at the chance to give her a break."

Shaking his head, Pearson glanced out the window behind his desk and then turned to me. "She wants to do this?"

"Yes, very much so."

"Are you sure this is what Ruby wants?"

"Yes." I folded my hands, praying, my eyes pleading.

"Go bring her inside. It's too hot to make her wait in the heat. But if she breaks my camera, it's coming out of your pay."

"You won't regret this. I promise." I ran from his office, elated at the opportunity.

Pearson yelled down the hallway. "Don't make promises you might have to break."

I called back. "No worries. Thank you."

**

I pushed the door open, looking up and down the sidewalk. "Ruby?" I spun in a circle and checked my truck, which was parked in front of me. "Where are you?"

From behind me, Pearson asked, "Where did she go?"

"I don't know. Ruby told me she loves to take pictures. She rode over here with me. She was ready to take on a job."

"And she has my camera?"

"Well, maybe…" I sighed, moving toward the bench by the window, noticing a bag beneath the seat. "Wait, this is her backpack. It's actually my blue one, but she didn't want to scuff the camera up and placed the Canon inside." I bent down. "The bag's heavy. She left the camera."

"See, how irresponsible. That camera's worth a lot of money. Someone could have taken it."

"But they didn't. It's safe. And I have it. I don't understand. Ruby wouldn't leave without a word."

"Seriously? You know she runs off when life gets hard. Even Earl and Max have said she can disappear for days. Maybe she's moving on."

I argued. "No way. She's not moving on. We're like sisters now."

"In less than two weeks?"

"Yes, life has brought us together. I've let her know she's welcome at the house. Something must have come up." I presented my validation of Ruby's character, but I knew she felt pressured to come with me this morning.

Pearson clapped his hands. "Get to it. Write me a piece that will change someone's life."

"I will. I'll get this for you." My mind wandered, and my mouth told Pearson what he wanted to hear. "I'll make some calls from my truck."

"See to it. You have the talent. But the focus is another thing."

"I won't let you down."

Pearson disappeared into the office, and I climbed into the truck, thinking about Ruby. I looked up and down the street for her. I wiped the sweat from my neck, the dampness on my collar, sticky like my life. I started the engine, letting the cold air blow across my face. Ruby's not been the same since I read her the letters from Daddy. Not since she discovered her dad saved me from the crash. She's distanced herself and barely spoken to me.

When I asked her if she wanted scrambled eggs for breakfast, she shrugged her shoulders and went to the yard. When I invited her to go with me to buy groceries, she shook her head, saying she was busy.

Just this morning, I pleaded with her about the job, so she could learn a trade and possibly make a career in photography. But right before we drove to the *Tribune*, Ruby screamed, "Sally, you're not in charge of my life. Stop telling me where I belong. Or what I'll need to do next. You're trying to fix my life again. Give it a break."

"But it's a job. It's an entry-level move. Give it a chance."

"You are relentless. What makes you think I need a job?"

"But how will you live?"

"I've lived fine without you telling me where to put the dish soap, or the laundry basket, or the skillet, or my empty glass. You're bossy, and you're acting like my dad now, when he was about to slam me up against the wall."

Her words caught me off guard. "Ruby, I'm not your dad. I don't hit."

"You do shove sometimes."

"I can be pushy. But you know I get caught up in things."

Ruby cried, her tears like a sack of trash falling from her childhood. "When I saw my dad's photo in the newspaper with you, the nightmares came back, and now I'm waking up shaking and jumping from the cot in fear. It's night terrors. I had them as a girl. And they're back."

"How can I help? Maybe a good bed to sleep in would help you rest?"

"I'm not sleeping in any of the beds in your house. I'm having a hard time with the idea that my dad saved you when you were a baby. He carried you to safety. Not me. He rescued you. Not me."

"But I didn't know it. I'm sorry your dad was not a good man."

Ruby swallowed hard. "My dad left my mouth bleeding and bruised when I didn't pour his coffee fast enough. Or when I didn't get his cigarettes from the nightstand. He hit me for looking at him the wrong way."

A lump in my throat gagged me. "I'm hurting for you. I can't imagine."

Ruby took a deep breath. "Staying with you is a rerun of the pain my dad inflicted on my mom and me. I'm not coping."

I cringed. "I'm sorry. Let me be your friend."

"I'm trying. I need some space."

175

"I understand."

Ruby shouted, "My panic and fear on the inside is larger than your kindness. I don't know how much longer I can stay."

"You must stay. I need you."

"You'll be fine. Your daddy loved you."

"But I could use your company and friendship. It's been years since I've had a good friend."

"I can't be your crutch."

"Crutch?"

"I'm not your rescue story. I'm not a cat you take under your wings to make your life better. We need to find ourselves, and we might need to go our separate ways."

"No, please. Come with me to Pearson's office. We'll get our new jobs started, and you'll get better. Then, I'll stop smothering you."

"Sally, the answer for me might not be the answer you want."

I begged. "Just come with me."

**

Well, now I'm sitting in the truck, and I'm wondering if I'm fit to freelance and write for the newspaper. And will I ever be a friend to anyone?

I looked at the list. "Dear God, let me take these names and numbers and write the best story of my life. I'll call these people and talk to each one. I'll let them tell me their passions and dreams and share their story."

I could almost hear Pearson responding with, "See that you do. I'm trusting you with a feature that should have gone to my seasoned reporter."

176

I whispered, "Thank you for trusting me with this."

I turned the air conditioning on high, taking my cell phone from the middle cup holder. I tried to get Ruby out of my thoughts, but all I could do was think about her. I dialed the phone. "Yes, I'm Sally Snow, with the *Tribune*. I'd love to visit with you today about a possible story we're doing. Can we meet for lunch?"

I pushed the speaker button so that I could hear the woman. She asked, "Yes, but what's this for, exactly?"

"My notes say you're involved in ministry at the prison, and you're close to the families who visit. You're Ms. Eden Welker, right?"

"I am. But I serve because God has called me. One of my sons spent time in jail, and I know how a family feels when their son or husband or relative is inside jail or prison."

"Can we meet at noon?"

"Yes, but I'm not your story. But I know who is."

I made plans to meet Eden at the local park, where I'd climbed the gym platform last week. "Thank you, I'll see you at noon."

I dialed the next person. "Hello, is this Larky Knightman?"

"Yes, that's me. I'm about to show some property. I'm a realtor. Are you looking for a home?"

"No, sir. I'm Sally Snow from the newspaper. I'm looking to write a story about a local hero. I understand you give to the homeless and have even bought bicycles for several of them over the years. And make secret donations."

"Sorry, the word *secret* is the key. I want to stay out of the limelight. I'm no hero." The speaker echoed Larky's response. "I could tell you who to write about if you'd like to know."

"Will you tell me his or her name?"

"No, but I'll be happy to show you."

"How about late this afternoon?"

"I'll meet you by the old jail on Farm Market Road 1840. Do you know where that is?"

"Yes, I think so."

I made one more phone call. "Hi, is this Roy Longly?"

My cell phone piped in with a man's voice on the speaker. "How can I help you?"

"I'm Sally Snow. I'm a new reporter with the *Tribune*, and I'm writing about local heroes. Can I make an appointment to see you?"

"You've got the wrong person. I'm not in the hero category."

"But I understand you volunteer to help people get their GED or find ways to search for work. You give of your time. That's a hero in my book."

"I do. But the hero you should write about isn't me. But I know one."

"Who might that be?"

"It's an unlikely person. She's seen but not seen. Heard, but not heard."

"It's a woman? Can you tell me who she is?"

"No, but I'll show you."

"How does four o'clock sound?"

"Perfect. Meet me at the corner of Merrill and Farm Market Road 1840."

"I'll be there." As I hung up, I knew that corner was the old jail that Mr. Knightman mentioned, the same place Mr. Longly wanted to meet. And I wondered what was up with that location.

Pearson stepped to my truck, and I rolled the window down. "I saw you sitting out here. You're wasting time."

"I'm not wasting time. I've booked three appointments in the last ten minutes. Each of them said something weird. They told me of another hero I should meet."

Pearson nodded. "Let's see where this goes. Sounds interesting." He wiped the bucket of sweat beading upon his face, and he ran his fingers through his curly hair.

I leaned closer to my dashboard, the cold air refreshing, and grinned. "You'd better go inside; I think you're melting."

"Get to it then. You're under a time crunch."

"I'll find you a hero. You'll see."

Painted Life

At the park, I stepped out of my truck and moved toward a woman with short gray hair, who held the hand of a young boy with wavy black locks. "Hello, are you Ms. Welker?"

"Hi there. You're Sally. I'd know you anywhere."

"It's the red hair. It gives me away every time."

"Well, you don't remember me, but my late husband, Gary, and I used to sit behind you at church when you were a girl. Your father always brought you orange slices to keep you quiet during the sermon, and our entire part of the church always smelled so good. I left church starving every Sunday."

"I don't even like oranges now. It's probably because I ate them so much as a girl."

The boy pulled Ms. Welker's hand. "Climb, I climb."

"Sure thing, baby. One second." She turned to me. "I brought my grandson, Keaton, so that he could slide and play. As for your story, I don't have much to say. But if you're searching for a hero, she shows herself on Friday nights at the old jail. Don't get in her way. She's a little cantankerous. But that's your hero."

"So, you're not going to let me write about you, are you?"

"No, but you'll find your story."

I grinned. "Thank you for talking to me, and enjoy your playtime with your grandson."

"I will. Maybe I'll see you at church."

"Maybe you will."

I hopped into my truck, took the winding road that cuts through the park, and pulled onto Merrill, heading south toward the jail. Parking on the street, I waited, nodding off for a bit inside the cab. Jerking awake, I checked the time on the dash, my truck still running. "Good, I didn't sleep too long."

The two-story red and white brick building covered the corner of the lot, and the main entrance, a wooden porch with rotten wood, didn't appear inviting to me. I marched down the walkway to the covered pavilion, which sat next to the newer gazebo.

I sat at one of the picnic tables, the heat scorching, so I marched right back to my truck, getting inside where the air cooled me. A white truck pulled up next to my passenger door. I pushed the button, rolling the window down, and the man opened his window too. "Are you Larky Knightman?"

"That's me. And you're Ms. Snow?"

"Yes, sir. So, tell me, why are we in this jail?"

"Well, these walls tell a story. We'll go to the south entrance, and I'll show you what I mean."

"Are we allowed to go inside?"

"I'm not sure. But many people do." He paused, holding the steering wheel with both hands. "You do want to write a story about a hero, right?"

"Yes, I do. And you're not letting me tell your story, are you?"

"No, I'm just a guy—nothing to talk about here. I love to give to others when God blesses me. But that's something we all should do."

"So, we're going to jail?"

"Yes, I've got a flashlight. What you see on the walls will change your life."

"My life? But how do you know what's inside?"

"Let's just say some of my giving happens here. When we go inside, the paintings will change you. Well, you'll need to see for yourself."

"Fine." I climbed from the truck, and we trudged across the overgrown lot, the weeds taller than my knees. "There could be snakes in this growth. Doesn't anyone mow the grass?"

"They do from time to time. But do watch where you step." The balding man, tall like Earl, marched in front of me. "Here we go, the door's cracked open."

Inside, we stepped over broken pieces of plaster and wood and what seemed like trash. "Mr. Knightman, it's not safe here."

"No, it's not, but you need to see the cells in the rear part of the first floor. The bars are still there, but the doors are gone. And please, call me Larky. My friends call me by my first name."

"Yes, sir." I stumbled over a pile of canvas on the floor. "What's this? Is that an easel we passed in the corner back there? And did I see paintbrushes?"

"Yes, she comes here to paint. Her sketches tell a story." We weaved down a hallway, the windows long behind us, and the flashlight lit our way. Larky stopped. "We're here. Do you have a camera?"

"I do, but I left it in the truck. I'm out of practice with covering stories. So let me run and get it."

"Hurry, I've got another appointment." Larky handed me the flashlight. "Take this; I know my way. Just pull the door closed when you leave. Don't miss the stories in the five cells. Look at the walls. And you'll see the hero in this town. The artist is a person who sees the broken ones around her. She helps those in need. If you want to know more, I'm sure Ed and Sammy may show up. They'll tell you how she cares for the lost and the lonely souls she meets."

"Who's Ed and Sammy? Are you sure I'm safe inside this building?"

"Let the walls talk. You'll see." Mr. Knightman slid into the shadows, and my curiosity sent me forward instead of back to the truck.

I came to the cell bars, and a glint of light showed me a part of the cell along the hallway. I pointed the flashlight. "What in the world?"

I marched to the far left, and the paint on the wall showed a girl of about five, with brown hair and blue ribbons in her pigtails. She was riding in a red wagon like I once rode in as a girl. And her smile revealed a snaggle-toothed grin, and her green eyes were familiar, like eyes I've met on a curb on a rainy night.

The wall also showed a man's muscular hand grasping the wagon's handle, the arm unfinished, and the person's body unknown.

I moved to the second cell. "I don't understand. Who comes here and paints?" The light from the barred window allowed the shadows to fall away, and the landscape of the next painting captured a garden of sunflowers. Some were taller than others, and the blooms were bright yellow with brown centers. The flowers held too many bumblebees to count. A girl, maybe the same one from the wagon but closer to twelve or thirteen, held a black kitten in her arms.

I knelt by the wall, shining the flashlight into the girl's face painted on it. "This can't be Ruby, can it?" I turned to get up, the air still, and a spider web stuck to my lips and eyes, wrapping around my head. "Oh, gosh! Stop, no spiders. I hate spiders."

I charged at the next wall in the third cell, still tasting spider-web germs. "Oh my, a wall painted with jars of jam.

Jars and jars. Red like strawberries. Blue like blueberries. And orange for peach, I guess."

I touched a painted jar on the wall. "Daddy, I miss you more than I can believe." Behind the painted jars of jam, from over the top of the maze, a set of eyes peeked out, the same green marble-like eyes as the girl's. But wait, a man's blue eyes with bushy eyebrows were painted on the wall too. I touched the eyes. "Daddy? Is this a painting of you?"

Ruby's longings were painted on the walls, capturing her heart. She wished for a father's love, and instead, her dad left her with emptiness and pain. I didn't realize how deep her wounds were, and how they left scars on her soul.

Stumbling, the tears ran down my face, and then I looked at the wall in the next cell with the same window as before, a hint of light let me see. On the wall, a man was eating ice cream in his recliner, holding an oversized bowl of vanilla ice cream. Next to him, sitting on the arm of the chair, a grown woman, Miss Ruby, held her bowl of ice cream too. The painting had them gazing into each other's eyes, as they smiled with contentment.

"I need my camera. This is unbelievable. But why would this make Ruby a hero? I don't understand."

I slipped down the hallway toward the last jail cell, and that wall sent me to my knees as I lost my breath. "I don't know what to make of this."

The final wall held a phrase beneath the painting, and the woman sat on a curb by a road, wearing a white hoodie. A gray cloud hung over her, and the girl's face was purple, as if she had bruises. Her lips seemed to have deep cuts, too, and the blood dripped down her chin.

Reaching for Ruby, the same arm, like in the first sketch with the wagon, held out an outstretched hand. The rest of the wall was a maze of paper airplanes flying in different directions. Some circling. Others were flying upwards. And the rest were sailing right at her.

I touched the wall, my fingers tracing the words by the young woman who again looked just like Ruby. I read the words three times before I could say them aloud. "Will you be my daddy?"

My throat was stuck with a glue of sorrow. I cried, "Where are you, Ruby Nell Collins? Don't run away. Please stay."

I hurried to get my camera, muddying the entire scene in my mind, confused and amazed at Ruby's talent. "How does this make her a hero? Or is she even the hero I'm after?"

Back inside, I rushed down the hallway with the Canon, shining Larky's flashlight to show me the way.

Kaboom-Dud.

A noise from the second floor stopped me in the center of the building, and I froze, unable to move, confident I wasn't alone. I shifted to the side, going into a room, crouching low, and I turned off the flashlight.

In seconds, voices from more than one person talked, but I couldn't tell what they were saying. Finally, I ran my hand along the wall to get closer to the hallway, and the conversation became clearer.

"I shut the door. I did." The deep baritone voice assured someone of the door's status. "Sammy, I promise. I shut the door. Stop getting mad at me."

"Ed, if we get found out, none of us can sleep here. You know there's about ten of us now, upstairs. Come on. I heard someone crying, and I saw a light."

"No one wanders over here except at Halloween. At least, that's what Ruby said. Hurry, let's check outside. If it's clear, we're good. Seth should be here soon with Roy. Seth said Ruby's been dealing with some family stuff this week, so he's bringing hot dogs and fries for supper. And Roy is dropping off some Gatorade."

Puzzled, I found myself wondering if Ruby painted the walls or if someone else did, but she sketched my smile. So I'm sure she painted the masterpieces. I took a deep breath, and another spider sent his web down my throat. "More spiders. I hate spiders." I yelled like a three-year-old trapped in the dark.

"Who's there? Show yourself." The baritone voice called.

"It's me, Sally," I responded with a timid voice. "I was hoping to write a story and got turned around. Can you show me the way out? I'm not here to cause trouble."

The stomping of bodies coming closer made me shake. "Who are you?"

"I'm Sally. Sally Snow. I'm friends with Ruby."

"Well, you should have said so."

From the hallway, a lantern lit the entrance to the room where all spiders go to make webs, and the sticky webs landed on my face. Yelling, I shouted, "I hate spiders!"

Mr. Baritone laughed. "So you've said. I'm Ed. And this is Sammy. We stay here. Ruby probably told you about us."

I flipped the flashlight on to add to our light. "Well, not exactly. We hadn't got to that part of her life."

Sammy spoke, his words lighter and less deep. "Some of us are passing through, and others have lived here longer. Ruby and Seth bring food, as do Mr. Knightman and Mr. Longly. They help us stay off the streets at night. Ruby is all about giving us scripture cards, too. She's a hero to us."

I gasped. "Ruby comes here. How many of you stay in this jail?"

Sammy piped in. "It depends. A few."

Ed sang with his voice. "If someone needs a spot, we've got a room."

I challenged them. "But you don't own this building."

"No, we don't. But it's abandoned. If you don't tell, we're swell.

I gulped, knowing I couldn't tell their secret. "But who painted the walls in the cells?"

Ed grinned, his yellow teeth in need of toothpaste, a brush, or both. "Ruby paints. She's an artist. Painting makes her happy. And if she's happy, we're all happy."

"So, Ruby's your friend?"

Sammy answered, "She gets us. She's family. She knows our troubles and helps us."

I shuffled my feet. "Can I take photos of the walls?"

Ed stepped in front of me. "I'm not so sure you should."

"Please, just for me. I won't show them to another soul."

Sammy wiped the web from his brow. "We can't let you give us away."

"I'm not. I just want the photos. The man in her drawings is my daddy."

Ed rubbed his chin. "She said Max is the father she wished for but didn't get."

From outside, a voice hollered. "It's time for supper. Come and get it."

Sammy rushed ahead. "That's Seth. We'll see what he has to say about your using a camera."

Ed motioned for me to come along, and I scuttled down the hallway to the door where Seth waited with sacks of food.

I tapped Ed on the shoulder. "Seth doesn't like me. Is there another door where I could just slip out?"

"Go back down the hallway, take a right, then a left. You'll find another exit there. But Seth will see you. He has eyes in the back of his head."

I turned on the flashlight, sliding along the hallway like a spider after its prey, and snapped several photographs of each painting. I went back, stepped to the hallway, taking the path Ed had given me, and marched out the door, only to run into Seth, who rounded the building. "What are you doing here?"

"I was talking with Ed and Sammy. I have an appointment to meet Roy Longly. He's helping me write a story about a hero."

"Roy's at the other end of the building."

"Let's go talk to him." I stuttered, "It seems this town could use a shelter for the homeless." Those words fell from my webbed lips before I could think, before I knew what I was saying, before I could swallow or take another breath.

Seth snapped his fingers. "And I suppose you'll be the one to make that happen?"

Heroes May Hide

I slapped my hand on the steering wheel. "Ruby, I've hunted for you for hours. Where are you?" I glanced up and down the street while sitting in the parking lot in front of the museum, facing the cafe. "Ruby Nell Collins, how can you simply disappear when life gets hard?"

Splat. Splat.

A blob of white droppings hit the windshield from a flyover of a late-night bird. "Thank you, Mr. Bird. You could have done that anywhere, and you chose the windshield of this truck."

I caught my anger rising as my words attacked an innocent bird doing what birds do. I then chuckled from my gut reaction to get mad. As for disappearing when life gets hard, I do that too. I've run away from my sorrow, and yet, I long for peace. And I could have come home when life was splatting ugliness my way, but I didn't.

For the last five hours, I've wondered about life and what I'm doing here, driving to and fro in search of Ruby. She's a constant irritation in my life, but I still enjoy her company. She's sketching friendship in my heart despite our arguing.

I've been tossed at her feet and in her path, and she's in my path. I know the help she needs, which comes from God. He's better at giving advice and guiding us if we'll let Him.

It's as if my own life's wanderings are playing out in Ruby. She's lost, and as I look in the rearview mirror of my journey, I'm lost too. But if Ruby looks for the northern star, maybe she'll find peace and discover where she should go.

Sighing, I sprayed the water mist on the windshield and pressed the wiper button, the goo washing away with wipe after wipe.

I put my head on the steering wheel, praying Ruby finds her sweet oasis of peace and that she's eventually led to where she is home. And I prayed, the Lord guided me. I need a sweet oasis too, and right now, I have no idea what that looks like for me.

Whining, I whispered to the hot breeze blowing across the cab from the opened windows. "Ruby, I've gone to the homeless camps in Texarkana and back to New Boston. Where are you?"

I clutched the wheel, holding the pain of Ruby's disappearance like a souvenir. I need to find her, but it's apparent she doesn't need me. Her sorrow and wounds run deep like the ocean, and she's caught on an island alone.

So far, no one's heard from Ruby, and now the moon's glow is reminding me I haven't eaten or gone home since late afternoon. Earlier, I stopped by the house, hoping Ruby had returned, and hungry cats met me. I noticed she'd folded up the blanket on her cot, and her pouch was gone.

I sat up, moving hair from my face, and ran my fingers across the top of the camera next to me in the passenger seat. I have Ruby's life captured in these photographs from jail, and I can't show anyone the photos. But oh, how I longed to share her magnificent paintings with the world. Her creativity, art, and imagery are a gift. I know she longs to be set free from her past.

I inhaled, my mouth drier than a desert, and my tongue felt like sandy granules. Licking my lips, I worried Ruby had no money and could use a drink or a snack. By knowing Ruby,

I've discovered a heartbeat of new life, and I have a desire to live with purpose.

Ruby's troubled as I am, and losing my daddy has taken its toll on her. It's taken my last bit of strength, too, and together we've lifted each other. But we've also railed at each other with our words, only to make up and recognize our ugliness.

I retraced my path from the gas station today, to talking with Katrina and Carl, to driving up to Jeanne and Ricky's house, who are back from vacation. But not one person has a clue. Or if they do, no one is sharing it with me. Instead, Earl encouraged me to give her space, to stop pushing her, and let Ruby breathe. Even Seth asked me not to get in Ruby's way, saying she's sorting through having Max love her, to not having him in her life.

Mr. Longly wanted me to see the paintings at the jail, too. He said meeting Ruby encouraged him to make a difference, like she does, in meaningful and purposeful ways.

I also learned that Ms. Welker makes hygiene bags for the homeless throughout the year, too.

Now I'm parked, keeping watch for any sign of Ruby in case she's out on the streets tonight. Also, in case she's waiting for Seth to leave his grandma's place or if she's headed to my house.

I wiped a tear as I took in the newness of Daddy's truck, knowing he would have loved having a new ride. My eyes welled up with tears, and my heart pounded, and I could barely breathe. But, maybe Earl is right. Space for Ruby. And space for me.

I dialed my cell, hitting the speaker button, and Pearson answered, "Sally?"

"Hi, I know it's late."

"Late? It's pushing eleven."

"Sorry. You need to assign this to another reporter because I can't write this piece. All the people I've spoken to today don't want recognition. So, I've got nothing." I coughed, choking on my sadness. "I don't think this is going to work out. I'm at a loss. Ruby's gone. Daddy's gone. I'm alone. And it hurts."

"Ruby's gone because she runs. She might show up, but give her a little room to figure things out. I know you miss your dad; he was one of a kind. We all loved him. I've never known a man with such compassion. He lived his life, and I hope to copy him. He was the sun in the garden of our lives."

I sighed. "Goodness, you're a writer for sure, the sun in the garden of our lives?"

"Yes, well, he was one of a kind."

"I know, my daddy was great. But I wasted time not being in his life."

"We all grow up. So don't beat yourself up. Some of us live in small towns. Others go on adventures into the city. But never forget, Max was so proud of you. As for Ruby, let her find her way as you find yours."

"Earl said the same thing about giving Ruby her space, and I have to agree. But I'm not sure what my space will include."

"You'll figure it out. Don't forget that next Wednesday, you have a booth to set up at Pioneer Days to sell your dad's jam. He would want you to set up for him."

"I'm not sure, I'll be here."

"Give the idea of leaving some rest. There could be a miracle in staying."

"Pearson, today I discovered Ruby is a friend to some homeless people at the old jail. She sees people others ignore. Ruby talks to those who could use a good conversation. She listens to them. But she's lost in her pain and needs a daddy."

"She's a person who loves the broken. And by the way, I know more about Ruby than I've told you. As for the people on your list to interview, they're in ministry helping Ruby love on those who pass through town. Each person planned to send you to Ruby's neck of the woods. Now, don't get me wrong, they are heroes in their own way, too."

"So, you set this entire thing up?"

"Well, I guess you could say that, but you needed to see with your own eyes. So, who did you talk to today?"

"I met Ms. Welker, and Larky Knightman, and Roy."

"Well, there are two more names on the list. Call them tomorrow. Let them point you toward home."

"I don't need to talk to them. My daddy's gone. And he loved Ruby. He saw her. He heard her. And he listened. I'm sorry, Pearson. I can't do life right now. I can't write a story."

"Maybe two more phone calls will change your mind."

"I'm not sure." I coughed; my throat was dry.

"Well then, let's write Ruby's story."

"So, there you go, making news out of her sorrow. She's not going to let you write about her. She's not even here. I can't find her."

"We could do her story and not share her name. Instead, we could use her servant's heart to boost morale in town and get people involved in living."

"Now, you're toying with me. You're just trying to sell newspapers," I grumbled, biting my lip before the side of me Pearson might not like exploded with words he'd wish to edit out from our conversation. I was close to splatting on him.

"Sally, I work for the newspaper. We know this is how I make a living. I sell papers, then I get to buy groceries. You write a story. And then you get to pay your bills."

"Stop trying to reason with me. I'm not in the mood to make a deal with you."

"I'm not making a deal. I want others to see your friend like you do, like Eden, Larky, and others. So, let's tell the story of a woman who hides among us, who has no family, no home, and who, how did you say it? Oh yeah, you said she's a friend to others."

"Stop it. You're pushing me into this story. How do I know you'll tell her story without sensationalizing it? Or exploiting her?"

"You write her story yourself. No editing on my part. If she's gone, let's tell our community about the hero that was right here, and they never saw her. I won't change a word. It's your baby. This is your moment to share her life with us."

I exhaled through my mouth and hoped I could genuinely show Ruby I cared about her. "Are you sure?"

"I'm sure. I'll give you the front-page feature. You get to use your words. I'll make sure the Chamber of Commerce is on board, and we'll give the honorary award to an *Unknown Hero.* That will be for our first award. What do you say? Let's do this."

"I don't know. This is way outside my comfort zone."

"Isn't this the kind of story you want to share? One that reaches the heart of the readers?"

"Fine, but do I have to finish by Sunday night?"

"Yes. A deadline is a deadline."

"But wait, I don't know what to write."

"You'll figure it out. I know you will."

Life in the Country

"Earl, it's me. Are you asleep?" I pounded on his door. "Earl, wake up."

The door creaked open, and Earl blinked his eyes, rubbing his ears with both hands. "Do you know what time it is?"

"Yes, it's six in the morning."

"Then go home."

"No, look at this. What do I make of it?" I handed him an envelope. "Look inside. There's a key. A key to … is it a key to the picture of this home?" I pulled out the photograph.

"Give me a second." He pondered over the photo, yawning three times. "Interesting."

"I'm sorry that I got you up. But I had to show you. Someone knocked on my door about four times, then rang the bell. When I got there, this was on the porch."

"I could have slept for another hour." He grabbed the envelope and made his way to the porch swing, wearing his favorite pajamas. "Let's see. A key? A two-story Victorian home? What could it mean?"

I plopped next to Earl, my head like a bird's nest, my wiry red hair poking out in all directions. "Stop this. You know something. I can tell by your voice."

"Go, get dressed. Let me show you." Earl handed me the key and the photograph. "This key is a sign of what your daddy planned, and the home in the photograph is a place he left for you."

"And you didn't tell me? Or think I should know? Nobody tells me anything."

"The prior owner had a delay in moving. So Larky told me he'd bring the key to you when they were gone. And with Max passing away, Larky was supposed to call me before he left you the key, to give me a chance to tell you about the house."

"This town has too many secrets. Too many. What am I to do with this big house?" I peered at the photo, the yellow siding, the white trim, a gazebo on the side, all pretty and inviting.

"Sally, those rooms will tell the stories of many people."

"What? I keep hearing everyone say rooms tell stories."

"You have a chance to share a home with people who need a home. As I said, get dressed. And comb your hair." Earl grinned, his hair sticking out over his ears.

"I'll be back in ten minutes. Give me a second." I charged to the house. Inside, scuffling across the floor, grabbing jeans and a shirt and my backpack and my cell, I grabbed the camera as if I might cover the story of my life.

I stood in my driveway. "Earl, come on. I'll drive. Show me where we're going, but I've got to make a couple of phone calls on the way. It seems I need to make a couple of appointments to meet two people for a story I'm working on for Pearson."

"Sure thing. You young people are attached to those cell phones. Give me a phone in the house, and I'll be fine. In my day, we went for hours without talking on our phones." Earl winked and climbed into the passenger seat.

Backing from the driveway, I put the truck into drive. "Where am I going?"

"Take Highway 82, west toward DeKalb. At Malta School, take a right, and we'll head north."

"Sure thing, but I need to get gas first." I'd left the list in the truck from last night and dialed the fourth name, putting my phone on speaker, but the call went to voicemail.

"Yes, please call me back; this is Sally Snow. My number is—"

Earl piped in, cutting me off. "Should you be talking and driving?"

"I can do two things at once. And I didn't get to leave a message thanks to you."

"You'll see. It's fine." Earl smirked, his words throwing more at me with his glances than with his words.

"What are you up to?"

"You'll see. Who else are you calling?"

"Well, the first call was to set up an interview with Mel Cantrell. I'll have to call her back. And the other one is Jillian Lewis. I expect Pearson has them in on his little plan, too."

"His plan?"

"Yes, he's having me interview people who are in ministry with Ruby." I bit my tongue. *Ouch!* "Wait, are you in on this, too?"

"I'm a friend to you. A dear friend of your dad's. And I love a good plot."

"Seriously, Earl. That doesn't even sound like something you would say."

Earl smiled. "But it sounds like something that Pearson might say."

I squinted, picking up speed down the highway. "You're in on it; this curious twist isn't without purpose."

"There is a design unfolding. And Max had hoped to be alive to show you." Earl pointed. "Gas. You need gas."

I pulled into the station, got out, and pumped the gasoline while Earl sat inside the cab. I shook my head, not sure what to think or what to do—Ruby's missing. I'm barely holding it together. And now I'm headed to a Victorian house with a key.

As we moved along, I pressed Earl for information. "Before I call this Jillian, just tell me who she is and who Mel is, and what they are to Ruby's story."

"You'll see. The loop of sorrow you've lived within is breaking free. Trust the ones in front of you now. There's Roy, Larky and Eden, along with Jillian and Mel. And you'll always have me by your side. But don't forget Pearson believes in you, too."

"So, you're all in cahoots. Small towns are full of meddling folks."

"This is more than meddling. This is destiny. And it's yours." Earl clapped his hands with two taps as if he would have loved to clap longer.

I turned the truck by the school, slowing down. "You're enjoying this, aren't you?"

"I might be a little thrilled. Treasures untold await you, wonders for your heart to behold."

I grimaced, unsure if his happiness was contagious or not, but somehow, I wanted more from life when I'm with Earl. "How far do we go down this road?"

"About another mile, then a right on a dirt road, and the house will be on our left, not far."

"I'm ready to know what you know, to get some answers."

"You'll see. Soon."

As I bounced in the seat on the dirt road, Earl pointed. "There's the house. Just like the photo."

I slowed the truck, the cattle crossing-grate slowing us down. "I have cows, too?"

"Cows. Chickens. A few horses. And a garden." Earl straightened up. "Look, the sign's up."

"The sign? Why is there a sign?"

"Read it as we drive up the gravel drive. Go slow. I want you to see it. Your dad named this place."

As I inched along the driveway, a small sign hung on a hanger. "Earl, it says *Sunflower Delights*. Was Daddy making this into a factory to make his jams?"

"Not exactly. It's a place to delight in, to see the sunrise. A home for the lost and the lonely."

"I'm confused." I swung the truck up the circular drive, coming up to another pickup like mine. "Is Pearson here?"

"Yes, he's waiting to see your face. And Jillian and Mel are here. The other two cars belong to them. They are your staff, and they're excited to work with you." Earl announced, seemingly confident I'd respond with joy.

"What? So now you're planning the rest of my life? When will I get a say on this?" I raised my voice, the shrill inside the cab, not one Earl liked since he put his hand up.

"Just walk with me. Take a stroll. See what your dad and Ruby saw in this place. See what they put into motion. Pray and see if the open door is for you. That's all. Just look. And listen to God speaking to your heart."

We climbed from the truck, the oversized porch winding to the left, and another similar Victorian-type house, smaller like a bed-and-breakfast add-on, sat to the right, near a barn. "So, there are two houses?"

"The main house has the kitchen and dining room for meals. The other house will house ten men, and the primary house will house ten women. This place is a sanctuary for those who need a fresh start. Who needs skills, guidance, and who needs a place to call home."

A tear leaked from my eye, streaking down my face like hope rising at sunrise. "My daddy put this into action. But how did he pay for this?"

"Your daddy sold jam, put every penny into savings, and never spent his money. Instead, he ate from his garden, and over the years, when food was about to get tossed at the cafe, Max brought meals home. The only splurge I'd say your dad had, well, it was his vanilla ice cream."

I chuckled. "Earl, so this place is paid for?"

"Yes, debt-free."

"But how in the world would I run this? I don't even have one check from Pearson yet. I'm broke."

"That's where Jillian and Mel, and Larky, and Roy, and Eden come in, along with the church. The support for this shelter is in place. The workers are ready, and they need a leader."

"I'm no leader. I'm barely a follower of anything."

"Well, you're not as broke as you might think. Your daddy left you some money at the credit union, enough to get you through for a couple of years. And his life insurance money will help keep this place going for a few years too."

I swallowed hard as we marched up the steps to the front door. "Daddy left me some money at the bank. But, hey, he left some for Ruby, too."

Before I could ask, Earl added. "Ruby transferred her part to your savings account. She did that the day after he gave you both money for vehicles."

"She left town without any of it?"

"Not exactly. She has a few hundred dollars on her."

I pulled on his arm. "So yesterday, you knew where she was? But Earl?"

"Ruby was confident of her decision. But she also knew you'd rush after her. She was afraid you'd talk her into staying and made me promise not to tell you."

The front door opened, and I looked out to the driveway as three other vehicles left a dusty trail behind them. "And who's that?"

Earl piped in. "That's Larky and Ms. Eden. I suppose that's Roy in the last car. We're here to support you. To help your dad see this ministry come together."

I sighed. "I'm not so sure. I have never done anything like this in my life."

"But Jill and Mel have; they've worked in shelters and with the homeless for years."

I paused before stepping inside, facing Pearson, who patiently waited for me to come inside. "This was my daddy's dream, though, not mine."

"But a dream from your dad can become a dream for you too." Earl countered, his words soft, so reassuring. "Take that walk with me."

Pearson greeted me. "Come inside, my friend. I hope that you're finally home."

In the room to the right, I noticed the walls. "Earl and Pearson, who painted these?" I swooped my hands in a circle, taking in the paintings of sunflowers in the frames.

Earl moved to a painting. "This is by your great friend and artist, Ruby Nell Collins."

I nearly collapsed. "Ruby painted these? Are they flowers from Daddy's garden?"

"Yes, Ruby used to sit outside with her easel and paint for hours. She fell in love with sunflowers."

I wept; the garden of my daddy's life was captured on the walls in a way that tells his life story. "Look, this painting has a paper airplane by the glass of flowers, ready for flight. In the second, a remote control, like my daddy's, so he could turn on the TV and listen to his sermons. And in the third, a jar of jam, strawberry with two sunflowers. One tall. The other giant."

I hurried to the third painting. "This is Daddy's wedding band next to the flowers on a table. And his watch. And his reading glasses."

From behind me, the shuffling of shoes told me a merry-go-round of people on a mission slipped in behind me. I took in a deep breath, turning around. "No way, you're the waitress from the Pitt Grill."

The heavyset woman, whose sweaty face glistened, smiled. "Yes, I'm Jillian Lewis. We met the other day before Ruby had her encounter with the rattlesnake."

I nodded. "You, small-town people stick together, don't you?"

"We do. But from what I've heard, you grew up here." Jillian laughed, her boisterous bellow loud enough to be an alarm. "It looks like you're a small-town girl too."

The small, petite woman next to her stepped up. "I'm Mel Cantrell. It's nice to meet you. I've heard such great things about you from Max."

"So, you knew my daddy?"

"I met him during his years of service at the shelter in Texarkana. Kindest soul I've ever met. I'm pretty sure I met you, too, when you were in middle school. But that was ages ago." She wiped her eyes, her nose tiny, her cheeks rosy.

"I loved my daddy. So much. You'll have to tell me more."

Mel grinned. "I would love to sit down with you. He was the funniest man with fishing stories and tales about you."

The room began to dance as if I had vertigo, and my sight blurred, and I put my hand on the wall. The moment grew in intensity, and my heart lost its rhythm. I suddenly felt my throat closing, my heart throbbing, and I charged from the living room, down the steps, and to the truck.

I barreled into the cab, breathing hard, and sweating—and panic took over. I couldn't handle the idea of running a shelter. It was too much to consider right now.

Earl rushed to the porch as the others piled out behind him. I rolled the window down. "I can't do this. I know you all mean well, but I just can't make any decisions. Not yet!"

Friends and Heroes

I yelled, "Can't a girl get some sleep?" I rolled over in my bed, kicking my backpack on the floor, along with the last four days of clothes I'd worn.

I marched to the kitchen, peering out the window to the backyard, where all the commotion took place. "What? Sammy and Ed? What are they doing here? And Seth?"

Storming to the porch, I pushed open the screen. "Hey, what are y'all doing?"

Seth carried a crate of jam. "We're loading up the bed of your truck. Pioneer Days will begin tonight, and I've put your two tables in the back and the canopy. I found a couple of lawn chairs, too. Sammy and Ed are helping you get ready for your booth. We're placing different kinds of jam in the crates from the shop. And as you sell out, we'll bring more to you."

I ran my fingers through my tangles. "To set up? I haven't left the house in almost four days. I'm not about to work a booth. I don't have the energy. And what makes you think I'd sell out of the jam?"

Ed marched by with his crate, placing it on the ground. "Your ad in the paper will raise money for the new home, *Sunflower Delights*. He smiled. "Ruby would be so proud of you."

"Wait, I never ran an ad. What did it say?"

Sammy ran by and came back from the shop, carrying a paper. "Right here, it's a fundraiser at your booth. It says you're selling the jam on your dad's behalf. All the proceeds will go to the home in the country."

Meow. Meow.

Snowball, along with Charcoal, circled my legs, rubbing up and crying with meows from their hungry bellies. "You're both starving." I turned to Sammy. "I never ran that ad."

Inside the kitchen, I grabbed the cat food from beneath the sink. And before I could pour the dry chunks, the bag slipped from my grasp, pouring out and onto the linoleum.

Since the kitties had tagged along, they quickly devoured the morsels, and I bounced back outside. "Seth, stop this nonsense. I'm not running the booth. I'm not doing this. Not for you. Not for the house in the country. Not for any reason."

A female voice rose behind me. "Will you do it for me?"

I twirled around in my sweats and Daddy's oversized T-shirt, and my bare feet felt the stickers of the dead grass jabbing at them. "Ruby Nell Collins?"

"Hi, I'm back for Pioneer Days. Earl invited me. I still need the wiggle room, but he mentioned how you'd locked yourself away. Earl figured you might need some help." Ruby grinned, her hair cut and groomed into a bob, and her jeans and pink top fresh and new.

A sticker poked my toe. *Ouch!* "Your hair? You've cut it."

"I love it. My auntie flew into Texarkana two days ago so that we could fly back together to her house. Once she saw me, she thought the dead ends should go. I've been staying at a hotel with her by the mall, and our flight was this evening, but then Earl called her." Ruby touched her hair, her smile sparkling like a new hope for my pity party.

My heart smiled with hope. "You look great. Gosh, it's only been a few days. But it's like a thousand sunrises, and sunsets have come and gone."

"I'm sorry for leaving as I did. I should have told you. But old habits are hard to break. I'm here now. I'll be your hands and feet if you'll let me. Let me help you as your daddy helped me."

I sobbed. "Thank you. With you coming back for Pioneer Days, that's the best present ever. Ever."

Sammy and Ed stomped by, putting crates into the truck. And Seth ran to Ruby, wrapping her into his arms. "Ruby, you're a sight for sore eyes."

"Stop. I come and go. You're used to it. And get off me. Someone might think you're sweet on me." Ruby hollered, scolding Seth, but by her smile, I saw a different story.

I watched; my eyes caught in the beauty of more than a friendship unfolding in front of me. I spoke, interrupting their moment. "Seth, I'll get my keys to the truck. If you will, please take the jam and the other items to our booth. I'll get dressed and walk over. I'll run the booth with Ruby's help."

Ruby jumped next to me. "I'll come inside and wait for you. We'll walk together."

As we jaunted into the house, Ruby's gasp made me stop. "What a magnificent job you've done here. I leave, and you don't do dishes anymore?" She pointed to the stack of cereal bowls in the sink.

"I've slept some. I couldn't seem to function."

"Interesting, you used to spend your time getting on to me for leaving my glass out, or a knife, or a spoon. And in this short time, you have cat food dumped on the floor, and you haven't taken out the trash, and the dishes are dirty. And you've folded a million airplanes and tossed them all around the living room."

We stood in the maze of paper planes. "I've been a wreck. I'm overwhelmed. The landscape of my life has taken on so much change. I'm not sure how to process where I am and what's next."

"I understand. Earl told me you saw the house in the country, the one which Max bought."

"I guess he told you I left them all standing there and that I ran away."

"Yes, we're both pretty good at the running part. Maybe, it's time we tried to stand in one place for a while."

I picked up an airplane. "Does this mean you'll stay?"

"It means I'll live with my auntie. But we'll be friends for life. And I'll see you. And if you want, you can come see me too."

I grabbed her by the neck, hugging Ruby. "I've been sad for so long, and I'm afraid to smile for too long."

"Let's just smile for today. Tomorrow has enough sorrow." Ruby pulled away. "Okay, enough with the touching."

"Sorry, it's hard for me not to hug."

Ruby giggled. "Hey, did you see the story Pearson wrote about Max?"

I lost my breath. "No, a story about Daddy?"

"Yes, he's the hero the Chamber of Commerce selected for Pioneer Days. In the story, Jillian shared his work at the shelter, and Mel added some comments. And Larky and Roy had kind words about Max. Along with Ms. Eden, Earl, Ricky, Jeanne, and some words from Seth, me, Sammy, and Ed. Your dad was a hero to many people, going about his business and showing kindness. I'll forever love him."

I wept as the sorrow gave way to joy in how my daddy quietly touched lives in our small town. He'll be the hero to my heart, always.

Rushing outside, I called. "Hey guys, where's the newspaper? I need to read the story about my daddy."

Seth motioned. "Over there. Sammy tossed it to the ground by the chickens."

"Ground? I'll need a frame for this story. I'll save it forever." I charged to the paper, picked it up, and on the front page was an old photograph of my daddy. "Look, it's when he was tending to his sunflowers. It's the summer when he grew one so big, the stalks grew higher than six feet. And the blooms were huge."

I crossed my legs and sat down on the ground, holding the paper in front of me, crying like a girl of two or seven or thirteen or even thirty-eight. I read the piece six times before my eyes cleared enough to take in all the love wrapped in each paragraph from friends.

Glancing up, I caught Ruby with a pad. "What are you doing?"

"I'm sketching you and the sunflowers. I may paint you someday. You never know."

Seth rushed by. "Keys. I need keys to take this stuff downtown."

"Oh yeah. I'll be right back."

I charged into the house, and for a moment, I saw a glass of sweet tea next to the remote on the end table by Daddy's recliner. And for half a second, I heard my daddy say, "Sunflower, I love you. Let's eat some ice cream later."

Ruby interrupted my daydreaming. "Keys. Seth is begging for the keys."

"Sorry, I tend to get lost inside this house. Good memories live here. These walls have stories."

She grabbed my arm, spinning me around. "So, it's true. You've been to the old jail?"

"Why do you ask?"

"You said the walls have stories. And that's what I told your daddy when I painted him into my life."

I stepped back, not sure if I was getting ready for a tongue-lashing or not. I shared my take on discovering Ruby's artwork. "Pearson first wanted me to write a story about you. And how you're a hero for this town. He sent me to Larky, Ms. Welker, and Roy. They all sent me to jail to learn about how you love the homeless, and that's when I met Sammy and Ed, well, after I saw your paintings."

"You don't know?" Ruby took the keys from my hand, turning to leave.

"Wait, don't say that and walk off."

"Read page two of the paper, down at the bottom. The city has fenced off the corner around the old jail and locked up the building. This is because too many folks are trespassing on the property."

"But where will Sammy and Ed and the others stay?"

"You know where. You hold the keys to life in the country. To a place where brokenness can turn to wholeness. Where sorrow can rise and grow into joy. Where the past can't go, where hope can live."

"Why does everyone think this is my destiny?"

Ruby spun around, kicking a pile of airplanes. "Look, you've landed back in your hometown. Every door is open for you. You have people around you who can offer more help than you'll need. You also have the money. And you have the house. You are the one who can change not one life, but more than you've ever imagined."

I shook my head so hard, my hair slapped me in the face. "It's easy to give advice. You're leaving. You're going home. You're taking your memories and making a new life."

"And you're trashing up your daddy's house and hiding out, for how long? How long will you feel sorry for yourself? I would give anything to be you. To have grown up in this house. On this street. With Pastor Earl next door. With sunflowers outside. With jam for breakfast. And ice cream at night. With someone to fish with. Do you hear me? Anything!"

Ruby stormed off, taking the keys and leaving me standing in the airplanes of my sorrow. I dropped to my knees, and Snowball curled up next to me, purring like he knew my pain.

"Snowball, what shall we do? Do you think we could ever live in the country? And is it possible I might be a leader after all?"

Meooowwww. Meooowwww.

I rubbed my cat's ears, his purr a sweet reminder of how precious friends and family are to a soul. Snowball rested in my arms, and I, too, rested in the return of Ruby, and in the story of my daddy in the paper. I've missed happiness and delighting in small things like a cat's purr or a helping hand. But could I ever be the daughter my daddy believed in?

Too Hot Not To Care

"Seth, we've sold every jar from the dining room and most of the jam in the shop. And people aren't asking for their change. Some even added more money to their purchase. I've lost track of what's come in for *Sunflower Delights*."

I ran my fingers around the lid of a jar and relished in the memory of Saturday morning's parade from earlier. Everyone came out for the marching bands and floats, and those activities brought plenty of patrons to the booth.

The last day of Pioneer Days is fast approaching the end; the mudding with four-wheelers ended this afternoon, the quilt show awards were given, and the endless array of events offered fun for everyone.

Ruby and I held down the fort at the booth along with Seth when he wasn't cooking at the cafe. Sammy and Ed kept us stocked, and Earl encouraged us with his stories of festivals past.

Seth wiped his chin of sweat, the dirt smearing across his face, a mark of his hard work. "I promised Max I'd come through for him. I sure wish he could see how good I'm doing."

I nodded. "He would be proud to know you were committed."

Seth straightened a row of jam. "I'm trying to keep my promises these days." He reached under the cloth covering the table. "We need a few more jars of peach jam on the table."

"Thanks. Maybe we'll run out before the night ends."

"We have a few jars in the shop, but those are for the cafe. Good thing you've found the recipes inside your dad's trunk. Jillian and Mel love canning and hope to keep making jam."

I heard myself say something I never thought I'd say. "We might turn making jam into a business for *Sunflower Delights*."

"I've told Earl I'll cook meals for you, on days when I'm off, if you need me."

"Well then, I'll need to pass on my daddy's chef hat to you so that you can wear it at the café and at the shelter."

"No, ma'am. I can't take your dad's hat."

"Don't call me ma'am. I'm your age. And yes, you'll take the hat or else."

Ruby spoke up. "Don't fight with her. You'll lose."

I tapped the top of a jar lid. "That's right. I tend to get my way."

Seth smarted off. "You tend to make your way happen."

"I can be bossy. Bossy can be good."

Ruby shook her head. "Bossy is not good. Not good at all. Just ask the dumpster at the gas station."

We giggled as the late-night settled in, as the band for Saturday night ramped up, as the country music pounded along the runway in the air. All around us were other vendors with crafts. With shirts for sale. Even a booth with an author. And yes, plenty of homemade gifts.

The Ferris wheel lit up the sky to our left, its orange and blue lights twirling as the wheel spun, along with other rides like a merry-go-round, swings sailing through the air, and mirrored mazes. I've walked through many mazes of lost steps and have no desire to go inside such a contraption.

The giggles of children racing ahead of their parents made me smile, and a memory of my childhood, running down the runway with my daddy, came to mind. Adults strolled back and forth, and I've waved at Larky five times. And each time he's holding a corndog. I'm not sure if he's eaten five of those things or just carrying the same one.

The entire community has rallied downtown, laughing, living, and loving each other throughout the hottest festival in Texas. But I'm sensing the current of my sadness turning into a heartbeat of new life. Things might get hot, but my faith in a new beginning is at hand.

I turned to Ruby, who rested in the lawn chair, her face sunburned, her eyes red, and her smile larger than a merry-go-round ride. "Hey, sleepyhead, I can't believe how much jam we've loaded onto the tables, how many have sold. I'm thankful you stayed. You made this possible. I needed you."

Coughing, Ruby jumped to her feet. "The jam's a hit this year. It might have to do with the hero award for Max, too. He would be thrilled to know that his jam is in the kitchens of most homes. Hey, I think I'll get another snow cone. I'm hotter than a grilled cheese sandwich in a skillet. Do you want one?"

"No, but I'd love another lemonade. Here's my refill cup. If you don't mind, get me a corn dog too."

"Sure, I'll get yours. I'm the errand girl. You'll miss me when I go to my auntie's tomorrow. I've brought you a lemonade on Wednesday night, then Thursday, and two on Friday. And today, you've gulped down five of them. You're spending our proceeds."

I grinned. "If I pass out from this heat, you'd be sorry. It's just lemonade. And I've counted six snow cones for you. So don't go pointing any fingers."

"Well, we should have brought bottled water as I said, but again, you know more than I do."

Laughing with my heart, I nodded. "Well, it's about time you recognized how much I know."

213

Ruby took my giant plastic cup. "It's August in East Texas. You don't have to be smart to know it's hot."

"You're going to miss me."

"I will. I'm not sure why. But I will."

Our eyes locked, two women with purpose, new opportunities unfolding like the emptying of soot from the chimney of one's past. "Ruby, you've changed my life, you know that, even if I had to shout at the dumpster to get some of my ugliness poured out when we first met."

"You were a little crazy that night."

I nodded. "I was stressed. My stress explodes loudly sometimes."

"You've got the loud part down."

I marched around the back of the booth, taking in the lights, the stream of cars rolling in for the final concert. "Hey, Ruby, who's the guy over there? He's hung out for the past hour next to those picnic tables close to the trash cans."

"I'm not sure. But he's not from here."

"Ruby, it's not like you know everyone. Hundreds of people come to Pioneer Days from all over the county."

"He's a wanderer. I can tell."

"How can you tell?" I stood next to her, cocking my head, gazing at the man who barely looked grown.

"He just picked up someone's cup left on a picnic table and took a drink."

My feet itched. "I'll go talk to him."

"Well, don't try the approach you used with me. Be his friend first. Let him know you see him. Tone down the eyes, no piercing glares." Ruby gave me marching orders, something she's great at doing, and I tugged on Seth's arm. "Hey, watch the booth."

"Sure thing. I've got it covered."

Ruby sighed. "I'm getting my snow cone and your lemonade, and yes, the corn dog."

"Get two corn dogs. And another lemonade." I offered my marching orders, too.

"Do I look like I can carry all of that?"

"You'll figure it out." I popped across the grass to the four picnic tables. "Hi, I'm Sally Snow. Can I sit across from you?"

"Sure, it's a free country."

"I couldn't help but notice that you took that cup after someone left." I put my hand to my mouth; so much for my improved technique with making an excellent first impression.

The young man pushed the cup aside. "The lady left an entire real Coke. Couldn't see wasting it."

I almost laughed when he said it was *real Coke.* "Good point. Have you had anything to eat today?"

"Nothing yet. I'll get something later."

From behind me, Ruby rushed up. "Hey, Sally. They had a special on corn dogs. Two for one. I've got yours, but now I have an extra one."

The man staring at the corn dog licked his lips. "Wasting food is never good."

I smiled. "So, I've heard. Would you like a corn dog?"

The man stood. "I've got to be going."

Ruby handed me the corn dogs and jumped beside him. "Can I hug you? You look like you need a hug."

I swallowed hard, unable to process how Ruby offered a hug to a stranger but struggled to hug me. She wrapped her arms around the man's neck before he could answer, or run, or duck.

"Ma'am, please. No touching."

I watched as the role reversal unfolded right before my eyes. I interjected my two cents. "So, what's your name? Please, sit with me. Ruby's headed back to our booth to get my lemonade. And I promise not to hug you. But I do have an extra corn dog."

Ruby scratched her ear. "Sure, back to the booth. My work is never done." She stormed away, but her half-grin told me she understood.

"So, what's your name? I'm not sure you answered with Ruby interrupting with her hugging and touching."

"Chris. I'm not from here."

"I grew up in New Boston. As small towns go, this is a good one. So, where's home for you?" I pushed the corn dog across the table to Chris.

"Texarkana. I've heard there's a place I might stay out here. But I don't know who to talk to or where to find this shelter."

"What sent you to the streets?" I pried, unsure if too many questions would run Chris off.

He took a bite of the corn dog, tears welling up in his eyes. "I'm missing my baby. He's two months old. And I can't see him."

"You have a son?"

"Yes, his name is Marcus."

I stuttered, glancing back at the booths and lights behind me, hoping for the right words. "So, can you answer this for me? Is there something you've done that made it impossible to see your son right now?"

Chris choked on the battered crust. "Yes, I made bad decisions, and my wife won't let me come home. I want to fix them, but it's going to take time."

"So, you want to find your way home?"

"Sure, I want to go home more than anything. But right now, I'm not able."

"Let's see if we can help you make that happen. Would you mind helping me at my booth? I'm selling jam and raising money for the shelter, the one I believe you are looking for in New Boston. Let's work together and figure out your next steps."

"But you just met me." Chris challenged me with his words. "You don't know anything about me. Why would you trust me?"

"We all make mistakes. You didn't sit behind my booth by accident. God sent you here. Let's see what He's up to with your life."

"But I could be dangerous."

"Or you could change and do good with your life."

"I would like to do good." He whispered his words.

"Do this for your son. And let's make him proud of you."

Chris reached across the table. "See this tattoo. It's for my mom. A couple of years ago, when she died, I got this sunflower tattooed on my wrist in her memory. My mother loved sunflowers."

I cleared my throat. "My daddy loved sunflowers too. Come on, let me introduce you to Seth." I pointed at the booth. "There's Earl and Sammy and Ed, too. I have a feeling you're about to meet some friends you'll have for life."

Jam on the Shelves

We walked across the grass toward the runway, where life abounded, and lights flickered. And right above the booth in the sky, a star sparkled like a spotlight of hope. Somehow, I knew Chris was our first resident at *Sunflower Delights*, that is, if you don't count the other eleven who moved into the shelter this week.

Chris stopped walking before stepping beneath the canopy. "Are you sure I'm welcome?"

I smiled. "Trust me. You're the guest of honor tonight."

"Thank you. I do need a place to stay."

From behind Chris, I heard a kitty crying and skipped around him. "Is that a kitten in your backpack?"

"Yes, he's a baby. I found him next to a dumpster, and he ran from me into the road. But I saved him from the car turning at the corner. The driver never saw him. So do you like cats?"

"I love cats. I grew up with them. I have Snowball and Charcoal now. Maybe I need a new kitten. What color is he?"

Chris unzipped the backpack, and two teeny blue eyes stuck out, the kitten welcoming me to his world.

Meow. Meow.

I reached for the furry thing, and his rough tongue licked my hand. "Oh, my word. He's polka-dotted with black and white specks. He's adorable."

Ruby bounded over. "No way. Now there's a cat for you. What crazy coloring." She petted his head. "So, a silly little kitty shows up tonight. Interesting timing."

I nodded. "It's perfect." I cuddled the kitten up to my neck. "I think he's special. And so does my daddy! I'll call him Sunflower."

Seth argued, "But what if he's a she-cat?"

Chris smiled. "Somehow, I'm not so sure Sally cares."

Earl shuffled up with popcorn in his hand. "So, who's our new friend? Could this be the handyman I'm looking for?"

Chris shook Earl's hand. "Yes, sir. I might be. I'm pretty good with a hammer, or tilling in the garden, and even better at tending to a yard. Just put me to work."

Ruby slugged my arm. "See, if we'd started with a handshake, maybe, I wouldn't have gotten stitches."

I mouthed, "And maybe I wouldn't have this scar."

Meow. Meow.

**

A red-faced man with black hair, wearing a long-sleeve dress shirt and slacks, strolled up to our table. He picked up a jar of jam. "Hi, I'm looking for Sally Snow. Is she here?"

I stepped up, cuddling Sunflower. "Hi, I'm Sally. How can I help you? Are you someone who likes peach or strawberry jam?"

"Well, I do like your father's jam. I'm here to make a proposition. I own Smith & Hall Markets in Texas. I'm Jackson Smith. Whenever I come through New Boston, I stop at the café on the corner. And I always leave with a jar of jam Max made. I'd love to visit with you about putting your father's jam on the shelves in my stores."

I coughed at the offer floating in my ears like a breeze of opportunity. "What? Daddy's jam?"

"Yes, you're his daughter, right? We'll make it worth your while. You'll have a say on the process and the ingredients. And we'll stick to his original labeling. And I'm sure the jam will sell great. It's tasty and sweet, and I know there's a secret ingredient. So do you have someone who speaks on your behalf, or do I talk to you?"

Ruby mustered her way next to me. "You'd better talk to Sally. She's bossy. She must have things way. Or she'll throw a fit. And she must have order and perfection too, whichever comes first. I promise if you make her daddy happy, then Sally will be your very best friend."

I laughed. "Yes, talk to me. But do let my manager, Earl Milton, in on this adventure. And Seth and Ed and Sammy. And yes, Ruby. And even my new friend, Chris." The kitten wiggled in my arms, meowing. "Oh, yes, and even little Sunflower might have a say in how this comes together."

Mr. Smith passed me his card. "I'll call you next week and set up a meeting."

With that, the country music stopped, and Pearson's voice blared over the intercom. "Friends, we have an announcement tonight. The inaugural award for New Boston's Pioneer Days Hero is at hand. The award goes to our great neighbor and friend, the late Max Williams, a man after God's own heart, loved by everyone. A man whose sunflowers grew taller than most. A man whose jam is the best. We love you, Max Williams. Sally, come pick up your dad's trophy and plaque. We'll have them at the Chamber booth."

A roar of praise rose in cheers from the crowd, all along the runway, with hoots and hollers, all for my daddy. He was a man who loved with his actions, like we all should, with gentleness and kind-heartedness.

A tear slipped down my face, and I smiled at Mr. Smith, and my heart burst with joy. So much has changed in such a short time. And thanks to Earl and Daddy and even Pearson, I'm home.

I soaked up the love exploding like fireworks beneath the canopy, knowing my days of throwing a fit in the garden and shouting at dumpsters were over. But I'll never let go of vanilla ice cream! Or this new kitty! Or my friendship with Ruby Nell Collins!

I handed the kitten to Ruby. "Hold this little thing."

"Sure, I'm someone you can order around. Anything else I can do for you?"

"No, not right now." I grinned, bumping her with my shoulder.

Ruby kissed Sunflower's head. "It's a good thing I like cats."

I handed Chris a piece of paper from my satchel. "Here, make an airplane. Send it sailing."

Chris held the paper, his right eye raised higher than his left. "Seriously, make an airplane?"

"Yes, my daddy believed flying a paper airplane gave you time to think about soaring into your day with hope. So come on. It's your initiation to move into the shelter."

Ruby shook her head. "Chris, she's a little crazy, but don't worry, Sally's not dangerous unless... unless you don't make that airplane for her. She means what she says and says what she means."

Earl yanked the paper from Chris. "Sally Snow, leave this boy alone. You'll run him off before he's had a good night's sleep."

I chuckled. "Sorry, I was hoping for a paper airplane tonight. Daddy did win the hero award, so we needed to see one fly."

Seth folded the paper after taking it from Earl. "Here, paper airplanes make me feel better. They help me remember Max and the night he saw a different flight plan in me: doing good, which was more than I knew was possible. Also, Ms.

Ruby Nell kept after me, and she now makes those silly airplanes, too."

Chris grinned. "I might need a piece of paper myself. God only knows what Sally sees in me."

I slapped Chris on the shoulder. "See, you get me. I'm just a small-town girl whose daddy looked for her, and she finally came home. You'll be home before you know it, too. Besides, you're right, *God only knows* what's hiding inside of you, if you'll trust Him with your walk."

Earl hugged me from the side. "Who knows, you may teach Sunday school one day with all that wisdom inside your head."

"Earl, you know I can't teach a class at the church. We've talked about this."

Ruby cackled, "Never say, never."

Orange Slice of Praise

Our crew from *Sunflower Delights* filed into the sanctuary for Sunday service. I sat between Seth and Earl, while Sammy and Ed slid next to Chris in front of us. I smiled at the size of my new family, even if some of them twitched and wiggled in the pews.

Obie and Tony, along with Nancy and Dana, added new drama this week, but Earl reminded me earlier to remain calm, point them to Christ, and encourage them to be a light in the community.

Now, as the fifteen or sixteen residents settled into their seats, squirming, nudging each other, and whispering about who knows what, Earl tapped Chris on the shoulder. "Let's show reverence when in church."

I whispered to Earl. "Seriously, you could have just said be quiet."

"I'm a pastor at heart. And old school. A sanctuary is a place to show reverence to God."

I nodded, knowing arguing with Earl is a waste of my time.

The organ and piano piped music into the church building, a signal for service to begin, and the worship leader stepped to the pulpit. I've grown up in this church, running in the hallways, learning Bible verses, and spitting at boys. I've even played hide-and-seek inside the baptistery. Well, at least twice.

This is my first time inside the sanctuary in years, and I'm without my daddy. A part of me longed for Ruby to join me, too, but she's painting, living with her aunt, and finding her way. I'm planning a trip to see her next month.

Sniff. Sniff.

I wiped my eyes; the sweet smell behind me made me turn. "Hi, Ms. Welker. I see Keaton's with you today."

"Yes, we should train up our children in the ways of the Lord."

"What's in the baggie?"

"Oh, orange slices. Keaton loves them."

I wiped a tear. "Can I have a slice?"

"But you don't like oranges."

I grinned. "I've changed my mind."

"Let me get you one."

She passed me a slice of orange, and I crammed the fruit into my mouth, the juiciness of my childhood a flashback to the sweet-and-sour flavors. But this morning, the sour trumped the sweet. *Yuck!*

The bit of orange made me spit, cough, and choke, and I gagged on the stringy part of the fruit. *Yuck!* "This is horrible. Just terrible."

Seth moved away from me, my wiggling bothersome to him. "Sally, we're in church. Stop being a nuisance."

"But this orange made me gag."

Earl bumped me. "Sunflower, sing along. And stop eating in church. A little reverence, please."

"Sorry, I needed a slice of orange so I could pretend Daddy gave it to me."

From the pew in front of me, Chris looked over his shoulder, grabbing his neck. "What's this? Sally, does this chewed-up orange belong to you?" Tossing it my way, the slice landed on Earl's fluffy hair, but he didn't notice; he was busy singing.

I raised my eyebrows, reaching for the piece of orange, only for Earl to growl, "What are you doing?"

I folded my hands, clasping the slimy gunk. "Nothing, nothing at all."

Chris chuckled, "Sally's in trouble."

Earl snapped his fingers. "You two, hush."

I giggled. "I love how church smells like my daddy."

Earl mumbled, "Will I have to send you to the nursery?"

I leaned against Earl's shoulder. "I'm a grown woman, remember?"

"Then stop acting like you're three."

From behind me, Ms. Welker handed me a tissue.

I whispered, "Thank you."

Earl shook his head, his foot tapping, and he resumed his singing with the congregation. "Turn your eyes upon Jesus, look full in His wonderful face, and the things of earth will grow strangely dim, in the light of His glory and grace."

I listened to the squeaky tone coming from the skinniest man at church, but when Earl praised God, I couldn't help but sing along. "…turn your eyes upon Jesus, look full in His wonderful face."

Earl ran his fingers through his hair, smiling at me with eyes of kindness. He whispered, "It does smell like Max in here. A fragrance of hope is upon us."

The sanctuary overflowed with high notes of praise, and Pearson's singing stood out in the choir loft. He gave me a wink. For some strange reason, I had the urge to run away until Earl wrapped his hand in mine, leaning close. "It's great to have you home."

The pastor sent us to our Bibles, and I cracked mine open, glancing down at a sketch I'd tucked inside the book of Proverbs. Ruby had mailed me a drawing, and she used colored pencils to give me a glimpse of the painting she's creating for my bedroom wall at *Sunflower Delights*.

The sketch showed me standing next to Daddy in his garden. And he's a young man. I'm around six with a yellow daisy in my hair, and I'm holding a polka-dotted kitten. Daddy's smiling and cuddling Snowball—and the sunflowers are towering high into the sky.

Next to Daddy is my mom, Marilyn, pretty and fair—happy and alive. She's holding onto the water hose. And Ruby's there too—she's around eight years old. She's peeking from behind a sunflower and holding onto Charcoal.

Earl is in the sketch too, skinny as ever, and much younger. He's clutching his Bible close to his heart. And the inscription on the bottom of the sketch reads: On Front Street Heroes Are Grown.

Smiling, I offered a prayer to God, "Thank you for Ruby, and for placing her in my path and for placing Ruby in front of Daddy's truck and in his garden, even if she took a few strawberries. I've received the sister I've always prayed for—but she's a little harder to control than I wished, and mouthy. She has too many opinions, which I'm sure is why you sent her my way. We're both a little needy and hard to manage. Which makes us absolutely perfect for each other."

Earl interrupted my prayer. "Amen. And amen."

I whispered, "Was I praying out loud?"

"Yes! But it was a great prayer!"

Chris turned around, giving us a sly grin. *Shh!* "A little reverence in church would be nice."

Books by Pam Kumpe

Annie Grace Kree Chronicles Series
1 Untied Shoelace
2 Unknown Soul
3 Rescue of Undaunted Spirit
4 Unwanted Sidekick
5 Unwavering Hope
6 Unshackled Courage

More Books
Rescue at Three Sisters Springs

See You in the Funny Papers
A Scoop of Inspiration

In the Lick of Time
A Goat with a Tote
Hattie Holmes Holds Her Breath

Rehab Ministry
Things I Learned in Jail
From Court to Christ

Homeless Ministry

My View from the Bridge
My View from the Street
My View of the Heart

www.pamkumpe.com

www.ingramcontent.com/pod-product-compliance
Lightning Source LLC
Chambersburg PA
CBHW022044240626

47154CB00007B/2563